Fiona Tarr

The Jericho Prophecy

Book 1

The Eternal Realm

Books by Fiona Tarr

The Covenant of Grace Series

Book 1 – Destiny of Kings

Book 2 – Seed of Hope

Book 3 – Legacy of Power

Book 4 – Heir of Vengeance

Book 5 – The Ehud Dagger – Prequel Novella

The Eternal Realm Series

Book 1 – The Jericho Prophecy

Book 2 – Delilah and the Dark God

Book 3 – Reign of Retribution

The Priestess Chronicles Series

Book 1 – Call of the Druids

Book 2 – Relic Seeker

Book 3 – Shiloh Rising

Foxy Mysteries

Book 1 – Death Beneath the Covers

Prologue

The Goddess gathered the energy from the matter around her and imagined what she wanted to see. Her Oasis, her Sanctuary formed before her sight and it was beautiful with fresh flowing water, lush green grass, precious creatures and an abundance of peaceful energy to fill her spirit.

The Host of Heaven was in disarray and Asherah withdrew from their divinity. Her sanctuary hovered above the new city founded by the exiled ancestors of creation. They were cursed for such a trivial transgression and the Goddess took pity on them vowing to protect and care for them until the end of time.

The people worshipped Asherah, goddess of fertility, love and nurturing until the reign of their civilisation became blinded by wealth and power and intelligent design, but the Priestesses of Asherah never lost faith for they were givers of harmony and healing.

War was coming to her people, Asherah could feel it in her spirit, but the wars of humanity passed quickly for the Host of Heaven, busy with a war of their own: a war that transcended eternity, a war that found no winners and continued to wreak havoc on the inhabitants of the world below.

 Chapter 1

The young woman wiped the table with her stained rag. Another night of heavy drinking patrons, bottom pinchers and foul innuendo was finally over. She threw the now soaked cloth over her shoulder, trying to ignore the waft of stale ale that filled her nostrils as she carried the last of the mugs, four in each hand to the wash room.

Despite the foul smell, she had to thank the Goddess Asherah for each day of freedom she enjoyed. It had come as quite a shock to her family when she had insisted she would leave the confines of their home before she married. Yet the real astonishment had occurred when she had shared her excitement over opening her own establishment. An Alehouse was not exactly considered reputable work and this was exacerbated by the fact that it was somehow always assumed that any unmarried woman who lived alone was a whore, selling herself for money to make ends meet.

The fact she did choose to bed the occasional handsome soul from time to time and that they often reciprocated with generous gifts was moot. She had never needed to sell herself to survive. In truth, her little establishment had turned out to be quite the profitable income earner.

She finished washing the mugs and left them on the counter to dry, wiping her hands on her apron before removing it and hanging it over the back of a rustic old hard wood chair she seldom found the time to sit upon.

'Thank you Musaf. That will be all tonight.' She smiled at the cook as he nodded his agreement and turned to leave.

She heard the front door slam as the wind whirled in and the cook left, but the sound of voices drifting into the wash room raised her curiosity. She poked her head out around the corner to see if Musaf had forgotten something.

'What did you miss this time?'

Instead of seeing her cook in the dining room, she was met by two young men with wide eyes and suspicious expressions.

'Sorry. We are closed.'

'Do you have rooms for the night?' Rahab stiffened as the man spoke. His accent was unfamiliar and he was obviously struggling to speak the local language.

'Did the man who left just now see you?' The two men looked questioningly at each other and shrugged. 'If he did, you do not have long before the guards arrive.' She ushered them into the back room, past the sink of drying dishes and around the corner into the alcove that housed the cooking stores. There was an open window that led onto the outside wall of the city of Jericho but no rear door.

The men looked at each other. The woman's reaction was not what they were expecting and neither of them was accustomed to being man-handled by a serving girl in such a way, but it was the shorter who appeared the most concerned as he spoke.

'I do not understand. What is wrong?'

'Oh, you mean apart from the fact you are obviously foreign and the city watch is on the lookout for Israeli spies.' Rahab looked squarely at both men and waited. It only took a moment before they looked away, trying to find a place to disappear into the cracks in the heavy stone walls. 'I have worked too hard to get where I am to get caught with spies in the midst of my business. You need to hide before the guards arrive.'

'This is your establishment?' The taller of the men, with dark almost black hair and the deepest brown eyes drilled her with his gaze. It made her both excited and uncomfortable at the same time but that did nothing to abate her reaction to his words.

'What! A woman cannot own an alehouse where you come from?' Rahab placed her hands on her hips challenging him to say what he was obviously thinking. Instead he grinned sheepishly and shrugged.

'We have no alehouses where we are from, but you are correct, if we did have them, a woman would not be running one.' Rahab waved her hands erratically in both apprehension of the guards who would likely turn up any minute and her own frustration at men in general.

'Climb this rope. Get to the roof.' Rahab reached out the window and pulled a heavy red cord through into the wash room. 'The roof top runs alongside the battlements so hide under the thatch or the guards on duty will see you. Do not forget to haul up this rope before you hide. I will tell the soldiers you have moved on.'

'Why?' The young man with the beautiful eyes asked.

'Because I am not one to help men die and if the guards get a hold of you, you are as good as dead.'

Salmah pushed Deshaun to the window ledge and nodded to indicate his friend should head through and do as he was told.

'The Lord our God will bless you for this.' Salmah smiled his thanks back through the window as he hung from the rope and began to follow his companion up to the rooftop.

'I follow Asherah and she loves all mankind, so this is your lucky day.' The young woman called to the retreating man. She considered his eyes again and shook herself back to reality as the door to her main room burst open.

'Where is the manager?' A gruff voice called out as tables and benches were pushed around, the scraping noise caused Rahab to rush into the dining room.

'What on earth is going on? I am the owner and I am sorry gentlemen, but my establishment is closed for the evening. My cook has gone home.'

'Yes, he came to the guard house and advised you had some unwanted guests. He claimed they were foreigners. If you are harbouring spies you will hang.' The Officer had a scar on his left cheek and a grizzly looking beard with flecks of silver revealing his age.

'I harbour no spies Officer. Two men arrived as Musaf left and I sent them on their way immediately. As I said, I am closed. They mumbled something about heading back toward the river along the Jordan road.' Rahab cast an unhappy eye around the room as the soldiers continued to upturn tables. 'Now please ask your men to stop making a mess or next time they want ale, they will be paying double for it. You understand!'

'Well you will not mind me just having a quick look around. We would not want anything untoward happening to you now would we Rahab?'

'Be my guest, but please do not break anything. Your men have the subtlety of rutting goats.'

She stepped back and allowed the Officer to walk through to the wash room. Like most of the local guard, he knew her well, but she could not remember his name. She carefully peered over his shoulder to see the rope had disappeared and slowly released the breath she had been holding.

The soldiers turned over every piece of furniture, looked in every cupboard they came across and even climbed the ladder to her loft bed, lifting the covers and throwing them down to the lower level as they searched.

'Satisfied?' Rahab scowled at the man in charge.

He nodded, but then walked over to the window on the outer wall. He poked his head out and looked up and down while Rahab held her breath once more. She forced herself to relax her expression as he turned back to her. 'Heading for the river you say?'

'Well that is what I heard. If I were you I would not be wasting any more time. If the King finds out you lost them, we might find you and not the spies hanging from the nearest tree.' Rahab smiled her most polite smile and walked to the front door, opening it wide so the guards could leave.

'Very well whore. I will be back personally to serve out your punishment if you are lying.' The smirk that slipped across the man's face left no room for misunderstanding and Rahab wisely chose not to point out that she was not a whore. It would make no difference to such a man.

It was a common misconception of the Priestesses of Asherah. It seemed women who worshipped the gods historically had no purpose except to be whores or concubines. Such constraints were placed on women by men and their carnal desires. There was not a man alive who could not imagine women sharing their bodies with each other and for that reason they judged the purpose of the Priestesses of Asherah was pleasure and nothing more.

Rahab waved the men out and placed the bar across the door. She leant against the closed door, somehow hoping to keep out further intrusion before taking a deep breath and giving up a silent prayer to Asherah.

Chapter 2

Uriah listened to the officer of the guard make his report and approved their pursuit of the spies. As he watched the troop leave he wondered again why the Israelites were sending spies and how they intended on crossing the Jordan with such a large company of men, women and children.

The Prince felt no need to share the news with the King just yet. His father was otherwise occupied. His latest concubine was a vision of beauty and Uriah had to admit he found her rather difficult to resist himself. Her long golden hair was unique amongst the local women and with her crystal green eyes she was nothing short of disarming.

Uriah shook his head to free his mind from the vision of her, yet he could not wipe the smile from his lips. He forced himself to focus.

The Israelites had travelled far and had not been heard of in nearly forty years. In that time, many tales had been told of their exodus from Egypt and the stories had ranged and grown in extravagance over the years. The fact that the entire population had gone missing, never seen or heard of for so long served to lead the Canaanite people to believe the whole story was just myth, especially the talk of the Prophet parting the Red Sea to aid in their escape.

Now, as they camped on the outskirts of the city of Jericho, questions were once again being asked and rumours were rife. What were their intentions? The Canaanite people were unsettled and the King had ordered the guards to be vigilant, hence the report of the Israeli spies.

Uriah wondered over where they had been seen. Rahab was well known among the guards and the senior officers, even the royal household and officials knew of her establishment. She was a strong-willed woman and was known to be a handful even at the best of times. Uriah could not help but anticipate trouble.

He swept up a mug of watered wine from his table as the guards left to continue their pursuit. The hour was late, yet the young Prince could not relax. Something felt wrong. When the second mug of wine did nothing to abate his concerns Uriah finally succumbed to the discomfort in his belly. He replaced his mug on the small table at his feet and called for his horse. He would take a ride out of the City himself and see if he could get to the bottom of why the Israelites lingered nearby.

****

'It has been such a lovely time Hamilkot, but I really must be leaving the Palace.' The woman's words floated in the air like clouds.

The King stood as his concubine draped the sheer golden fabric over her shoulder and tied it in a neat bow. Gently he stroked her hair and touched her almost luminescent pearl white cheeks. 'My dear, I am the King and I require you to stay. We have only just begun to get to know one another as intimately as I would like.'

The woman smiled with genuine affection. 'Oh Hamilkot,' she breathed 'you see, I have other commitments.'

'You are already married, betrothed to another!' The King took his hand away from the woman's golden hair as though he were avoiding a wasp sting.

'Nothing like that.' She turned without further explanation and left the King's chambers, her hips swaying seductively as she walked. He stared uncomprehendingly at her bare shoulders and perfectly proportioned body. He tried to speak, but the words were stuck in his throat as his thoughts began to wander. By the time the woman had closed the heavily carved wooden door, he had sat back down on his soft bed, surrounded by brightly coloured cushions and drifted off to a dreamless slumber.

Chapter 3

Rahab looked out her window and listened to ensure she could not hear the guards on the wall. She called up from the window. 'You can come down now.'

A few moments passed before the red rope uncoiled with a spring in front of the window, followed shortly by Deshaun, then Salmah.

The men slid into the wash room with ease and Deshaun wasted no time in heading for the front door.

'Where on earth do you think you are going?' Rahab stared at the young man.

'We have to report back to Joshua.' Deshaun's expression was confused.

'You need to leave by that rope.' Rahab pointed to the window. 'There is no way I can risk you being seen leaving my premises. I just told the guards you had already left.'

'Deshaun, you head back to Joshua. I do not think we have enough information to leave just yet. Besides, we owe this woman our life. I think it only right that she be protected.' Salmah smiled to his friend who replied with a frown of confusion. Why would Salmah wish to spend another waking moment in this city, with its foul-smelling streets and loose women?

'I do not need your protection.' Rahab stared defiantly at the young man.

'You do not get my protection; you receive the protection of my God.'

'Well if it is the protection from your God, I am sure He can provide it in your absence, but either way, I told you, I worship Asherah and she has looked after me just fine so far.' Rahab tried to ignore the wide smile and allure of his dark deep brown eyes. She deepened the frown on her face intentionally, not wanting to give him any sense he was having an impact on her.

'I am sorry, we did not introduce ourselves. This is Deshaun, I am Salmah.' Rahab stared for a moment. She did not want to know their names; they should have been gone already.

'Why are you still here?' Rahab offered a cheeky smile to soften her words.

'We owe you a lot. I want to stay to ensure you remain safe. Deshaun will return to our camp to give a report. Tell Joshua I need more time to investigate further.'

'What is to investigate? God has called us to this land. It is ours. We will take it.' Deshaun's confusion continued to grow.

'Oh wait up a moment. You need to take a breath.' Rahab raised her hand, finger pointed to the heavens and her pulse suddenly rising. 'We know a lot about your people. Stories about parting the Red Sea and all that, but what makes you think this is your land for the taking? There are people who live here you know. You cannot just take what you want.' Rahab felt her anger rising and she struggled to control it.

'Deshaun, head back to Joshua as I said. Tell him to do nothing until I return.'

'I am not sure I can convince him of that Salmah, you represent only one tribe of Israel.'

'Yes my friend and you represent another. See what you can do.'

'I will try.' Deshaun moved towards the window and took one last look over his shoulder before lowering himself into the darkness below.

Rahab's establishment formed part of the outer wall of the city and guards passed above her home on the hour, every hour. She hoped the spy would not be seen making his way in the darkness. She sat silently trying not to focus her attention on Salmah who watched his friend retreat.

'I am sorry. Deshaun is a little over zealous at times, well most of the time really.' Salmah grinned.

'Does he speak for your people?' Rahab tried to keep the fear and frustration from her voice.

'Well that depends on a lot. We have waited nearly forty years to make claim on this land.'

'We have lived here a lot longer than that.'

'True. The land was promised to us by our Lord God and He will see that it is ours. Will your people embrace a nation of refugees?'

There was a long silence as Rahab considered the question she already knew the answer to. No, the Canaanites feared the Israeli people. The history of friction between the two nations was old and outdated time itself. The stories of their miracles had spread long before she was born and they had been told and retold throughout her childhood. Even as she had worshipped Asherah, there was talk of the Israelite God Yahweh. It was said that Asherah was a lesser god of the heavens and had once been Yahweh's lover.

'Tell me more about your God Salmah.' Rahab was curious now. She had never met an Israelite before and learning of their god intrigued her.

'After you tell me your name.' Salmah grinned almost boyishly.

'My name is Rahab and you should know, I am a Priestess of Asherah and contrary to popular belief, that does not make me a prostitute.'

'I am not here to judge you Rahab. I am here to save you.' Rahab laughed then. A full belly laugh which caused Salmah to frown until he suddenly recalled the circumstances of their meeting and joined in her mirth.

Chapter 4

'Why has Salmah stayed behind? The house of Judah is constantly causing trouble in our progress. Always questioning the will of our Lord.' Deshaun stepped back from the grey haired old man who had led the Israelites into the Promised Land. His anger was barely in check and his hands shook with frustration.

'I cannot say with certainty, but he promised the Lord's protection to the woman. He believed he owed the prostitute her safety for without her, we would have been arrested by city guards. I have to agree, she saved our lives.' Deshaun spoke the last quietly, trying not to further anger the anointed leader of his people.

'The Lord saved your lives Deshaun, not some wayward woman.' Joshua growled and Deshaun took another half step backwards in retreat. Joshua composed himself and stepped forward to pat the young man on the shoulder as he continued.

'The Lord has spoken to me on this very evening Deshaun. We will leave to lay siege on the walls of Jericho at first light.' Joshua waved his hand to dismiss the young leader of the Levite tribe but when he remained looking on nervously, Joshua frowned. 'What is it Deshaun?'

'Well, I um, Salmah asked me to request more time. He believes that the people of Jericho might be saved.'

'That is not the Lord's will or Salmah's problem Deshaun. The Prophet Eleazar was clear. The walls will fall and all must die. Every man, woman and child who does not follow our God will perish. Now I will grant the prostitute Rahab and her family protection as Salmah has promised, even though it was without my approval, but we march on Jericho at dawn whether Salmah has safely returned or not.'

Deshaun could see there was no give in the old man. He had endured many years of hardship and it was well known he wanted to lead the people out of the desert and into the Promised Land before he died.

The young leader of the Levite tribe knew Salmah was not comfortable with the outright murder of an entire nation and sought to find an alternative. Dashaun could not help but feel the same way. Was it truly the will of God to kill an entire race to make way for another?

****

'You believe I am a whore?' Rahab's features were composed as she handed Salmah a mug of ale, removed her dirty apron from the chair and took a seat.

'That is not what I said. Do you always try to read the minds of people you barely know?' Salmah smiled as he took a deep drink of the ale. 'This is very good.' He raised the mug in salute.

'No, I do not try to read minds, but I usually can. Men are often very easily read.'

'Usually?'

'Yes, like your friend Dashaun.'

'Yes, well I agree with you there. Dashaun is very easy to understand. He is a Levite. They do not like to think outside that which they have been taught. He has never met a woman who is unmarried at your age.'

'At my age!' Rahab almost rose from the chair with the rising volume of her words.

'Forgive me Rahab, I am not saying you are old….' Salmah put his hand up defensively.

'But I am *that age*.' Rahab kept the smile from her face as she watched her visitor begin to squirm.

'I think you are enjoying this too much.'

'I am. I must admit though, you take more than the most average of men to become uncomfortable around me. I have always had that effect which is why I chose to become a Priestess of Asherah and open my own business. My family has accepted my choice with time and this place has been both rewarding and difficult. The women who work in my establishment are often treated as whores because we worship the Goddess, but they have remained unmarried by choice.'

Salmah watched Rahab as she spoke. She was not a traditionally beautiful woman with her close-set eyes and sharp features, but there was something about her that communicated without words and Salmah was drawn to her like a bee to honey.

'So, it is uncommon for women to remain unmarried here too?' Salmah wondered aloud.

'Yes, yet men can carry on as they please and unmarried women are all at their mercy. Is it different with your people?'

Salmah remained silent for a time. He wished in his heart that he could say it was, but it was not. The Israelites were a small population made up of twelves tribes and the women were married between the tribes quite young. Many young men had perished over the years of desert life before coming to Jericho. The older men had been left with the responsibility to build the tribe and so many young women had been promised into early marriage to old men.

Salmah had refused to take a wife until they were settled in the Promised Land, something that Joshua often berated him for.

'We have no unmarried woman.' Salmah knew it was not the response Rahab wanted to hear. Instead he changed the subject. 'Thank you for helping us.'

'You have already thanked me and I have already told you, I would have done the same for anyone. Our King is like most Kings, he wishes to keep power and as soon as word of your tribe entering our lands reached him, he had his soldiers roaming the streets for someone to hang.'

'We have no King other than God.'

'Yet you seek power.' It was not a question. Rahab softened her words with a grin. 'It is the way of men.'

'We do not seek power.'

'No? So it is only your God who seeks the power.'

'I do not believe it is power He seeks, I believe it is love.'

'Ah, a truly romantic invader then?'

Chapter 5

Salmah shimmied down the rope in the grey of the predawn. No soldiers had returned to do Rahab any harm and Salmah felt comfortable leaving for the time being at least. They had spent most of the night talking of God and Rahab had shared her belief in Asherah the goddess of nature. There was no doubt in his mind there were many gods for if there was only one, why would the God of Israel forbid the worship of other gods?

There was even further proof in their own history. The people had been aimlessly waiting for the Prophet to return from Mount Sinai when they had been tempted by worshippers of Baal. Their punishment had been severe and the situation only served to substantiate the existence of other gods.

Now as he pondered Rahab's goddess Asherah and her dominion over love, life and fertility, he could not help but wonder why the Lord of his people wished to kill all others. Surely it would be best to convince them that the Israelite God, was the one true God? Killing them all showed his power, of that there was no doubt, but where did it show His love and was His love reserved for His people alone?

Salmah pushed his confusion aside as he reached the ground and made for the treeline. The young leader of the tribe of Judah felt a growing need for clarity and Joshua was the only man alive who could answer his questions. It was he alone who was said to hear the word of the Lord. The prophets often saw visions, but visions were only slices of the truth and Salmah could not help but wonder if the will of man was mixed with the real intention and will of God in such prophecies.

Salmah's own thoughts frightened him for to air such ideas aloud would label him blasphemous. He wondered where the thoughts had sprung from, then he smiled as he recalled Rahab's words during the evening. *This all sounds to me like you have a war in Heaven and your god is asking humanity to take sides!* There were those who thought Rahab a harlot, but either way it mattered not to Salmah, he had to see that she remained safe in the coming invasion of Jericho and there was something about her inquisitive nature that he could not ignore.

****

Rahab watched the young man leave and considered trying to get a few hours of sleep before the Inn opened, but there were too many thoughts roaming her mind to rest. Instead she reached for her shawl and carefully covered her hair, pulling the fabric around her face. The early mornings were still a little cool and the grove of trees at the shrine of Asherah was always colder than anywhere else in Jericho for it was surrounded by tall walls that had been built over the years.

Rahab wondered if this made Asherah angry for the Goddess loved life and the fertility of the land was stifled by the many buildings and the growing city walls which cut out the sunlight that was the energy of all things.

The walk was not far and Rahab took a deep breath as she reached the shrine of Asherah. The statue of the Goddess was old and stained with bird lime and the weathering of years of rain. Rahab could not say how old it was for no one alive could recall when it had been erected or even by whom. Did the Goddess put it there herself? Was it carved from stone by her followers in the times when all worshipped the old gods of the land?

Rahab allowed her mind to relax with each deep breath she took. She knelt at the base of the statue and bent over to place her forehead on the soft grass that managed to grow even without sunlight. Its mere existence spoke volumes to the young Priestess of the power of the Goddess. Where else could lush green grass grow constantly shaded from sunlight if not at the temple of Asherah?

The predawn light slowly gave way to the early morning sounds of life. The birds began to chirp with the dawn as Rahab continued her meditation, focussing on each and every breath and the scent of life that manifested with every slow and steady draw of air.

I can hear you Rahab. I know your questions. Yes, protect the Israelites, go with the leader of the tribe of Judah. Jericho will fall, but I will be with her. Follow your heart child for your love with bring love and protection to the world like no one has ever seen before.

Rahab's vision flashed with pain and terror, blood and revenge but as those images faded, they were replaced with unfamiliar lands. She could see great tall shiny buildings with coloured glass and people rushing around in carriages with no horses to pull them. There were people feeding the poor on the streets and no one was left to starve or sell their bodies for food.

The Covenant of Law will fade and the Covenant of Grace will take its place but the road is long and it begins with you my child.

The words of the Goddess faded as the shrine came into full light. Rahab felt sad at what she knew was to come in the days ahead, but in her heart she understood that all change took sacrifice and that there was peace in knowing that the gods were real.

For if the gods existed, so too did Heaven and a life free of hunger and pain after the soul departed this land.

****

Uriah watched the young spy reach the camp of the Israelites and realised his men had been deceived. Someone had harboured them within the city walls after all and there was no doubt in his mind Rahab had something to do with it. Her confused devotion to the Goddess caused her to have an unrealistic view on how the world of power worked.

Uriah pushed the thought of Rahab aside. He would deal with her when he returned. His attention was diverted as he realised there was some sort of argument breaking out amongst the men in the camp below. He wished he could hear what was being said.

The spy who had just returned was waving his hands around and the old man with the almost white grey beard seemed to be unconvinced. The camp was already packed up and ready for travel.

There was some type of shrine — a golden box being carried on long thick poles with a group of men in ornate robes walking before it. The people slowly began to follow like sheep and Uriah wondered again how so many would cross the river Jordan.

Earlier in the night he had left his horse behind and travelled up and around through rocky narrow ground to cross the river. It had been a slow process with little moonlight to guide his way, but even by daylight there was no way that the Israelites were going to make their way through the narrow pass with their herds of livestock, carts full of possessions and so many elderly trailing along.

Uriah wondered if he should return to his father and report, yet something stirred in his spirit and curiosity got the better of him. He returned through the difficult passage and waited by the river, just below Jericho. Could the god of Israel perform the miracles the rumours had alluded to for all these years? Surely not.

The hours passed as the Israelites massed before the river Jordan and Uriah's stomach knotted with anticipation. The royal house of Jericho had long since given away worship to the gods. The ruling class considered the gods nonsense, yet they were the perfect tool to be used as the need arose.

The pantheon of Canaanite gods was extensive and the idea helped the poor sleep at night and motivated them to rise early and work hard throughout the day. The gods took the blame for the misfortune of the lower classes and could always be called upon to accept the responsibility of ultimate power when the rulers chose to put such a slant on their latest failure.

His father, the King of Jericho allowed the shrines of Baal, Anat and Asherah among others to remain, for tending them motivated the people, but the wealthy did not believe in such a naive understanding of the way of the world.

So, what would happen in Jericho if the Israelites somehow crossed the Jordan and attributed their conquest to their god? The results would be catastrophic to the Kingdom for the wealthy would grow petrified of anything with more power than them and the poor would grow unsettled with their own beliefs. Either way, he had to hope no miracles would ensue, but in whom could such a godless man instil hope? Uriah smiled at the irony and waited.

Chapter 6

'You will do as you are told Salmah. The tribe of Judah is one of the twelve tribes of Israel, but do not press me for we can make do with eleven.'

Salmah said nothing. There was no way to reason with Joshua. How could you reason with a man who had been appointed by God Himself to rule a people? He was beyond compromise. In everything he did he believed he was fully supported by the Lord.

The Priests did not rebuke him, the Prophets said nothing to dissuade him. No, whether God ordained it or not, no one would stand against Joshua as leader of the Israeli people. Not on this day.

Joshua walked past the young man and began barking orders. The Priests would start out, the Ark containing the stone tablet on which the law was written would follow, carried by the Priests of the tribe of Levi. All the people and livestock would follow under the direction of their tribal leaders.

If Joshua was right and he usually was when it came to the word of God, then the waters of the Jordan would be parted as the Red Sea had been generations before. Only Joshua and Caleb were alive to tell this story as no other man had been granted permission by God to enter the Promised Land.

Of the twelve spies who represented the twelve tribes of Israel who entered the land of the Canaanites and found that their fields were lush and their resources for growth many, only two could be allowed to enter the Promised Land.

God had sent the people of Israel to wander the desert until all those born in Egypt except Caleb and Joshua were gone from this world. With the last of them dead, now and only now were the Israelites to inherit God's chosen land.

It was said the spies had all lied about the fertility and prospects of the Canaanite lands for they had feared the advanced armies and forces of the lands of Canaan. Only Caleb and Joshua had told the truth and believed that God would deliver the land to them. It was said that because of this lack of faith all would have to wait and not all would see the Promised Land.

It had felt like a folktale for so many years and although Joshua had not given up hope, some of the remaining tribes had. The leaders of the tribes of Reuben and Gad had chosen not to enter Canaanite lands, for they believed the fighting and further war were not worth the sacrifice and were happy to stay where they were, east of the Jordan river.

Joshua had not wanted to agree, but eventually he did but only if the two tribes saw the fall of Jericho and all the remaining tribes could safety travel into the Canaanite lands to seek their future.

Now as they milled at the river, a sea of faces waited on their leader as he spoke. Joshua's words were clear in the ears of everyone all the way back to the last row of women and children, yet he did not shout.

'The Priests will go ahead and call aside the waters of the Jordan. Stay close and follow the Covenant of the Lord, but remember not to touch the Ark, for it is forbidden. You will all arrive before the walls of Jericho with dry feet, thanks to the promise of our Lord God. You will all bear witness to the miracle of His power and you will bow down before Him and only Him. You will kill all who do not believe for our Lord does not abide the following of other gods above Him.'

Joshua's voice returned to normal, no longer echoing throughout the tribes. He called the tribal leaders to him. Salmah and Deshaun stood together as they waited.

'As we cross, you will all collect up the largest boulder you can carry from the bed of the river. We will make a monument here to show the glory of our crossing. Generations to come will know what passed here today and they will honour the God of our people.'

Joshua took no questions and instead began to follow along with the Priests and the Ark. Salmah could not help but feel apprehensive. There was no doubt in his mind how powerful the God of his people was, but after the night before when he had spoken for hours with Rahab he had questions and they were not going to be answered from a show of power.

As soon as he reached Jericho, he would scale the walls to see Rahab again. He was concerned now about her safety and although Joshua had agreed to spare her and her family, she would need time to gather them to her before the people of Israel invaded the City of Jericho.

Try as hard as he could, Salmah could not force the bile from his mouth at what was to become of the people of Jericho. Surely if Rahab was a good person amongst her city, then there were others within the walls who saw the world as she did, with equality and love instead of rage and power.

As preoccupied as his mind was, all thoughts dissipated in an instant as the waters of the Jordan began to cease. The river did not flow fast at this time of year, but that took nothing from the display of power the people of Israel and Jericho were to bear witness to.

As the Ark and the Priests carrying it moved into the river, as soon as their feet touched the ground the river bed below them began to run dry and the water above slowly ceased to run at all. A low wall of water began to appear with every step.

As the Priests reach the centre of the river there was not a drop of water left on the ground and the sand had totally absorbed all the moisture like the wick of a lamp.

The people walked calmly past the Priests, giving the Ark a wide and apprehensive berth and passed out of the river bed onto the banks of the Jordan below the city of Jericho. As promised, not a man, woman or child had so much as a drop of moisture upon their feet.

Dashaun and Salmah stopped in the middle of the river along with the other young tribal leaders, including those of Reuben and Gad.

Salmah looked at the water that now stood above them almost shoulder high. He surveyed the river bed below and could see that no water even trickled further downstream. Dashaun looked wide eyed, almost fearful as he ducked down to collect up the largest rock he could carry. His eyes darted from the rock to the wall of water and back again.

'Can you swim Dashaun?' Salmah asked with a wicked grin. The younger man nodded nervously. 'Well, what is the worst that can happen my friend? We get wet!'

'There is a lot of water held back there. I do not believe I can swim that well.' Dashaun relaxed at the banter but did not take his eyes away from the wall of water. He studied the fish swimming within. They were oblivious to the lack of flow and seemed to be enjoying the additional depth.

Both men peered through into the water as though it were being held in place by an invisible transparent wall. Salmah was tempted to touch the water with his finger, but resisted the urge; instead he shook his head and began to walk a little faster. Unlike Joshua, his faith might be strong but it was not without its limitations and he was not about to hang around too long in case God decided, as Joshua had threatened, that he was not required in the new nation of Israel after all.

Each tribal leader had treated the selection of their offering as a competition, all trying to outdo each in their choice of the most magnificent rock they could find. Not one man had considered how many steps they would have to carry the rock and as they tossed their boulders to the ground at the banks of the Jordan all twelve young men struggled to draw air into their lungs.

Salmah lent forward with his hands resting on his knees, while Dashaun simply collapsed to the ground, rolling onto his back and holding his chest. Neither could speak.

As the remaining tribal leaders reached the banks of the river, the Priests began to make the final crossing. No sooner had the last Priest's foot reached the bank then the river began to flow once more.

Instead of a tirade of water bursting forth like a waterfall, the bottom of the wall began to trickle. The people of Israel looked on mesmerised as the little crevices in the river bed darkened with the moisture as it slowly ran along the ripples of sand forged by years of erosion.

As the water made its way down the river bed, the wall slowly lowered, the occasional fish flopped out the side of the wall of water, through the air and into the water below. No one moved until the river was once again level and slowly flowing down toward its place of rest in the Dead Sea.

Chapter 7

Uriah had seen enough. He did not wait to make sure the Priests of Israel carried the shrine of their god to dry land. His horse could not gallop fast enough for his liking. As he rode, tucked down over the mane of his mount, he thought of how he was going to punish Rahab for her protection of such an invading force.

'Close the gates. For the love of Baal, close the gates.' Calling on the old god would get those stupid guards moving Uriah knew. No one invoked the name of Baal anymore and if the Prince of Jericho was calling for divine help, they would be jumping quickly to the task.

Somewhere in his soul, even Uriah was hoping for some divine help, any help, in the midst of his sudden fear. How on earth were they to stand against a people whose god could stop the flow of a river in their path?

Uriah looked back to see the gates closing and the bar being put in place. From the vantage point of horseback, he spotted Nimal, the guard who had been sent to pursue the spies. 'Nimal, I know where your spy has been.' The man looked up and walked over to the Prince. 'Send word to close all the gates to the city. No one in or out without my order. I will speak with you before sunset. Meet me in my pavilion. For now, I must see the King.'

'What is it Prince?'

'I will explain later. No one in or out Nimal. You understand? It will be your head if you fail me.'

The Captain of the guard nodded and rushed to give orders.

Uriah wanted to go straight to Rahab and haul her out into the streets by her hair but she would have to wait. Her establishment was on his way to the Palace but he pushed the temptation from his mind. The King needed his report now, even if his new concubine was with him. Rahab was not going anywhere now that the gates were barred.

The ride back to the Palace felt like eternity and gave Uriah too much time to relive the memory of what he had just seen. How could anyone stop the power of so much water so easily? How was he going to explain what he had seen to his father?

The King would likely be angry that news of the spies was not brought to him earlier, but Uriah hoped the distraction of his consort would keep him in good spirits. He tried to recall her name but no matter how hard he tried, in fact the more effort he put into recalling her name, the harder it was to remember.

He convinced himself it did not matter. Either way, his father would deal with the situation in whatever way he saw fit. War was coming to their peaceful city and nothing either of them could do was going to change that.

As he reached the steps to the Palace, it appeared word had already spread. The guards were doubled and the marshalling yard was alive with activity. He was surprised to see his father was not already joining his men.

'Oh thank the gods you are back. We have been looking for you everywhere.' Jirad bowed deeply as he spoke. The man was head of the household and his expression looked alarmed to say the least.

'You have heard of the Israelite's approach I take it. Where is my father?' Jirad frowned at the Prince.

'No Sire. I called for the guards to be doubled for I feared the King has been poisoned.'

Uriah leapt from the back of his horse and tossed the reigns to Jirad who fumbled with them and then stared at the rough leather in his hands as though they were a serpent. He waved them above his head until a stable boy ran over to retrieve them. As he relieved himself of the horse, he took the steps as quickly as he could to keep up with the Prince.

Uriah stormed into the Palace taking the steps to the upper level two at a time. If anyone had poisoned his father, his new consort would have to know something. They had been inseparable for weeks.

He pushed open the double doors leading to his father's apartment and found all manner of mayhem. There were Priests of the old religion, physicians, servants and officials all huddled around the King's bed like a flock of birds.

'Everyone out!' All eyes fell on the Prince but no one spoke. The silence grew uncomfortable until Jirad caught up and walked in, breathless behind the Prince.

'You heard your Grace.' All moved as one toward the doorway, filtering past the motionless Prince as though he were a column in the middle of the room to be navigated around. Jirad waited for the room to empty and then checked on the King.

'Does he still live?' The Prince joined Jirad and touched his father's arm gently. It was warm and the King's colour was good.

'He does your Grace? It is most peculiar but he does not seem to be in any particular danger.'

Uriah was the oldest son and heir to the Kingdom but his father's business of running the City of Jericho had never stopped him from taking time with his children.

On the rise of the full moon every month, the sons would set out on a hunting expedition. It was a great opportunity to bond with their father and each other, yet it also served to rid the local village of any predators roaming the area seeking to kill live-stock. The boys always managed to find a lion, or desert cat causing mischief.

Uriah pushed his emotions down, suddenly recalling the imminent danger that faced his father's city. 'Where is the King's consort?'

Jirad shrugged. 'She left early this morning, before dawn I believe.'

'When did you find my father like this?'

'Shortly after dawn your Grace. I came to rouse him for the morning. It was unlike him to sleep late but he has been rather energetic of late.' The servant smiled a wicked grin and even in the pressure of the moment Uriah could not help but smile in return. The woman had certainly given him a new lease on life, one Uriah could not help but feel a little jealous of.

'She must know something about his condition and I wish we had time to search the city for her, but we have other more pressing matters to deal with.'

'What is the trouble?' Jirad raised a questioning eyebrow to the Prince.

'Call the King's Council. I need to speak with them. The Israelites have crossed the Jordan and will be before our walls by night fall.'

Jirad stared at the Prince for only a moment before realisation struck. 'Oh my!' He rushed off without further commentary.

Uriah looked at his father. He looked somehow happy, even content in his blissful slumber. No one had been able to raise him from his deep sleep and as Uriah touched the King's face, he could feel the man was still warm. He watched his father's chest rise and fall rhythmically and the fear he had first felt began to dissipate. The King was alive, but unconscious and in no position to make decisions on behalf of Jericho. The power and responsibility fell to Uriah and for the first time in his life, the young Prince felt less than confident.

Chapter 8

Salmah felt uneasy as they finally approached the walls of Jericho. The city sat upon a rise with high walls and square battlements surrounding the entire perimeter and offering protection to the population. The tribes had met along the journey from the river to the city and both he and Deshaun had explained what they had discovered.

The city had been built on top of a natural spring the local people called Ayn Al-Sultan. This was the lifeblood of the community and without it, all would perish. Salmah had been uncomfortable disclosing this intelligence to Joshua for he now feared for all the people in Canaan.

When he had first agreed to spy on the area including Jericho he had thought Joshua sought the means to make peace with the local people and buy or entice them to allow the Israelites to settle amongst them.

Now he knew that for whatever reason either Joshua or God Himself had chosen this place to make a point and put on a display of God's power. Salmah reasoned that it was likely the work of the Priest Eleazar or Joshua himself, for why would God wish to destroy life? But if it was not God's will, then why did He part the waters of the Jordan?

Salmah was so confused and a sense of unexplained shame was filling his heart, making him feel ill at ease. He needed to see Rahab. He told himself it was to secure her safety.

With a heart full of responsibility, Salmah found Joshua. 'I wish to return to Rahab, to help her prepare for the invasion and bring her family to her home. If we are to invade soon, she will need to have them all in one place so that our soldiers know to spare them.'

'You can return Salmah but do not think for a moment I have missed your true motivation.'

Salmah avoided the gaze of the most revered man amongst the Israeli people. He needed to do the right thing, no matter what Joshua thought. He did admit to himself that saving Rahab had become increasingly important since they had been apart. He missed her intellectual arguments and conversation of the gods and her love for her people. Most of all, he felt he owed her. She had been willing to risk herself to save strangers because it was the right thing to do. He wished that more people could be like Rahab and then maybe God would not need to attack the people of Jericho to make room for the Israelites.

'I will warn her of the dangers and ask her to assemble her family. Nothing more Joshua.'

'It matters not. The walls will fall on Jericho. Most of the people will die in the destruction and there will be very little need for our soldiers to kill anyone. Only Rahab's home will be spared the destructions.'

'What do you mean? Why bring the men of Reuben and Gad here if not to fight?'

'They came because God called them.'

'I thought they came because you threatened their families and their future.' Salmah was growing angry. What game was Joshua playing with the lives of his fellow tribesman? The old man had all but forced the Reuben and Gad tribal leaders to follow him to battle the Canaanites and now if what he said were to become true, they had left their families for no more reason than to make a point.

'Be careful Salmah. I said it before and I will not say it again. The Promised Land will survive without you or the tribe of Judah.'

Salmah only nodded. He was young and Joshua was old. For whatever reason, he held God's favour but no man could live forever. As he left the camp, Salmah felt his anxiety leaving him and his anticipation rising. Soon he would be able to see with his own eyes that Rahab was safe.

****

Uriah poured a mug of wine and considered sitting down after such a long and drawn out meeting of the King's council. Politics was the realm of his father and the young Prince had no taste for it. How on earth did the King ever get anything done? The factions had argued until the late afternoon.

At first, they had accused Uriah of imagining the whole episode, until the sun passed its zenith and the Prince had unceremoniously walked them all begrudgingly out to the ramparts and shown them with their own eyes the amassing forces of the Israelites almost upon the doorstep of their city.

It was then that suggestions and barrages of information had come spilling out of every corner of the room. There were talks of treaties, of negotiations and war. None present seemed to understand the significance of the power of the Israelite God. To part the river and allow his people to cross without so much as a wet toe was astounding to say the least.

Uriah shook his head as rage replaced his frustration. Rahab was the cause of all of this. If she had not harboured the spies, they would never have continued with their journey.

The Prince staggered from his quarters and bumped into Nimal.

'Your Grace, are you ready for me yet?'

Uriah frowned and tried to focus on the man, then realised he had planned to meet the Captain of the guard. 'Perfect timing Nimal. You can accompany me as we arrest the whore.'

'That would be my pleasure your Grace.' Uriah could not be sure but he thought for a moment the guard had licked his lips.

Chapter 9

Rahab was exhausted. She had not slept since the night before last and her fatigue was getting the better of her.

Musaf looked at the dark rings around her eyes. 'You should get some rest. You look like a mess. There will be no tips tonight with such a dark looking face. I will see to it the girls look after our guests.'

Rahab nodded and instead of heading to her loft bed, she took the rope to the roof. The cook thought nothing of it. He knew how much she enjoyed her solitude and the rooftop was often the only place a woman like Rahab could find peace.

Musaf continued preparing meals, washing dishes and planning the menu for the following day. He had worked at the Inn for many years and had grown fond of Rahab and the ladies who worked with her.

He knew that the Priestesses of Asherah were not common whores. They were women of power and purpose. They chose when and who they took to their beds and many high-ranking officials frequented the establishment. Even the Prince had visited from time to time and he especially had a soft spot for Rahab. It was because of this that Musaf thought nothing of Uriah's arrival.

He was only a moment away from calling up from the washroom to get Rahab's attention when Shiba stopped him.

'Something is not right Musaf. Do not call the mistress.'

Musaf peered out into the dining room and saw the Prince was indeed flanked by four city guards. As he pulled his head back into the wash room he nodded his agreement. 'They will hear nothing from me.'

'Thank you Musaf. I will cover for the Mistress.' The young woman brushed her dress into place and strolled casually out into the dining hall. There were dignitaries everywhere. It seemed the stress of the recent arrival of the Israelites had brought every man of wealth and status out for a little pleasure and relief.

'Gentlemen, your Grace. How can I assist you this evening?' The girl curtsied politely, allowing her cleavage to be revealed as she slowly lowered and raised her upper body before the Prince.

'Where is Rahab?' The Prince wasted no time. He was not to be distracted by the young woman's allure.

'I am so sorry your Grace. Rahab has taken the evening off. She has asked me to take charge tonight. I am sure I can find someone to look after you.' The woman smiled provocatively.

'Rahab has harboured spies and I will see her head on a pike. If she will not come forward now, maybe I should drag you out into the street as an example.'

The Prince could barely believe his own ears. He was not known for such violent behaviour but somewhere deep in his soul he was so angry he could not contain his rage.

'Please your Grace. I am sure Rahab will answer your charges as soon as she returns. Please, take a seat and enjoy some refreshments. You seem to be more stressed than usual.'

'Of course I am stressed you stupid whore. There is a whole nation of Israelites camped outside the city and it is Rahab's fault.' The Prince kept the news of his father's condition to himself. All the Palace servants had been sworn to secrecy on pain of death should even a hint of the King's misfortune leak to the public.

Shiba swallowed her fear as she spoke. 'Your Grace knows I am a Priestess of Asherah and that the Goddess has served our city well with fertility, love and abundance of crops for generations. Please, if you return to the Palace I will ensure my Mistress hears of your desire to see her beheaded and she will willingly answer your accusations.'

Uriah felt intoxicated but could recall only a few glasses of wine. He felt suddenly tired, as though a fog had been placed around him, restricting every movement. Something inside of him relaxed suddenly and he was ready to let the matter lie but he was too late.

Nimal grabbed the Priestess by the hair. 'What was it you said your Grace? You wanted Rahab dragged out into the common area by her hair. Well Rahab does not seem to be here to answer the charges, maybe this whore can do so in her place?'

Uriah made to object but he was not quick enough. Musaf appeared in the doorway, meat clever in his hand and a menacing look on his face.

'You heard the Priestess. She only works here. If you have cause to complain to the Mistress, we will ensure she gets your message.'

Uriah said nothing. His mind was racing and Nimal took his silence as permission to keep up his aggressive assault on the young woman. She screamed a gut-wrenching sound as the guard began dragging her out of the dining area. There were Officials everywhere, some Uriah had only just finished meeting with. He saw the scene unfolding like a bad dream and tried to force himself into some sense of reality.

He knew something about this situation was wrong, yet he was struggling for clarity. What was in his wine? For goodness sake, he had only downed one, possibly two mugs of the liquid. Why on earth could he not see straight? He raised his hand and attempted to speak, but the words simply would not leave his lips.

Musaf stepped forward, meat clever gleaming in his hand. 'When I came to you Nimal, you said that no harm would come to the woman of this Order. You only wanted information about the spies.'

'That was before that upper-class whore lied about the spies. That was yesterday, before the Israelites camped outside our city. The situation has changed.' The guard tried to defend his actions but the big man was having none of it. He knew the reality of why Nimal disliked Rahab and it had nothing to do with spies and everything to do with rejection.

'So, the Mistress did not accept your advances and now you feel hard done by. Wonderful! Such a strong and powerful exhibit of Canaanite manhood you are Nimal. Whoever put you in charge needs to have his mind examined by the physicians.' The cook goaded the Captain while the other three guards looked on in confusion. The Prince had not given the order to kill anyone and while the Prince was present, he was in charge. They all looked at each other with a sense of apprehension.

Nimal held the still screaming Priestess by the hair and drew his sword at the advancing cook as the room exploded in confusion. Officials stood, the Priestesses screamed or gasped and other patrons made for the door to leave. The Prince was dazed, trapped in a dream world he was struggling to escape.

'Enough!' The voice was strong and powerful and all eyes fell on Rahab as she entered the dining hall from the washroom. She had been blissfully asleep as the moon rose and the sun set upon the walls of Jericho when Asherah had come to her in her dreams.

Now, as she looked on the commotion before her, a sense of peace filled her heart as though she were viewing the scene from above or in retrospect. There was no emotion, no fear, just purpose.

Behind her Salmah had reached the top of the rope and entered the wash room unseen. He heard the Priestess shout and scurried across the room unnoticed by those beyond. Something was wrong he could feel it, but he knew revealing himself would only escalate the situation.

Rahab walked past the stunned cook and even ignored Nimal who almost growled at her presence. She looked absently at Shiba as she struggled against the powerful grasp of the man who held her with a weapon capable of taking off her head in one stroke.

She walked up to the Prince and placed her hand on his chest. The room fell silent except for the gasps of a handful. 'You know me Uriah. I know you. This is not your way.'

Uriah shook his head as if he had woken from unconsciousness. He placed his hand on Rahab's, which had not left his chest and held it there. 'You have betrayed us.' His words were softly spoken, with a sense of sadness.

'I have betrayed no-one my friend. We have known each other since we were children. When have

I done anything that was not born of love?' Rahab was unsure if the words were hers or Asherah's but either way, Uriah heard the truth of them.

'Nimal. Let the girl go.' His eyes were fixed on Rahab as he spoke and he kept his hand atop hers.

'But your Grace…' The guard shook the Priestess by the hair in protest. Shiba held the guard's hands in hers in an attempt to limit her pain.

'You heard me Nimal.' The words were spoken softly, but there was no doubt the Prince was not to be disobeyed. Nimal lowered his weapon and let the girl's hair go, but not before tossing her to the side of the room, knocking over chairs in her path. Two Priestesses rushed to her side, pulling her out of harm's way.

'Thank you Uriah.' The Prince let Rahab's hand go and left without another word.

Salmah had watched from the wash room and frowned at the look on the Prince's face. There was a tenderness in his eyes and a past he did not know, did not want to know. Rahab left the dining hall and saw Salmah as she reached the back room.

'When did you arrive?' She asked calmly.

'Just in time to see that.' Salmah indicated with his head towards the last guard leaving through the front door. 'How on earth did you managed to bring a sense of calm? I was sure someone was about to die.'

'I have no idea.' Salmah looked at Rahab in disbelief. 'No, honestly. I was asleep on the roof when Asherah came into my dreams. She was with me Salmah.'

Salmah could not deny someone was looking after the Priestess. 'Explain to me again what it is you do?'

'I am a Priestess of Asherah. I run this establishment. Do you want details Salmah?' Rahab's look was nothing short of challenging and although Salmah had more questions, he realised now was not the time to ask them.

Chapter 10

Asherah held back the tears that threatened to flow. She had felt the presence of Moloch before she had left the King in his dream world but now his influence was threatening one of her own Priestesses.

Uriah was not a man of violence and Moloch's power was growing if his influence was reaching the likes of the Prince of Jericho. Who else was being twisted by the demi-god that craved the life-force of children and why?

It had been necessary to take Hamilkot out of the situation. He was a seasoned politician and commanded one of the strongest elite armies in the region. If he had been awake when the Israelites crossed the Jordan many lives would have already been lost.

Uriah on the other hand was usually not so quick to anger but it seemed Moloch had been watching Asherah and making plans of his own.

Yahweh's plan was to bring the walls of Jericho down as an example of His power yet there was more to this scheme than mere men could understand and Asherah knew she was expected to play her part.

The history of Heaven was complex and the people could not hope to comprehend what went on beyond the stars. Asherah knew her worshippers understood snippets of her history, that she was a Goddess, a lesser god of Heaven, but that was an overly simplistic way Asherah had chosen to explain her place in history.

She longed to share the truth of her birth with her followers, but to do so would require a complex explanation of Yahweh and His place in creation and she knew to do so would confuse her Priestesses. The Order of Asherah believed they were all women because only women could truly know the depths of love, but Asherah knew that the God of the Israelites was love, a love to be shared beyond the Israeli nation.

The Goddess shook her head as she wondered if her followers would ever understand the extent of her place in the Halls of Heaven.

She pushed the thought from her mind and focussed on Rahab. The Priestess had been born under a blood moon, the symbol of the Goddess herself. Rahab's line would be the mother of Grace but before the prophecy could be fulfilled her descendants would birth the new Order and Asherah would be there to guide her children.

Asherah took a deep calming breath as she walked through the trees and soft green carpet of grass toward the shrine. The mist of the clouds floated in from beyond the boundaries of her oasis and the Goddess bowed momentarily before the marble pool of water.

'Oh Father, I wish you spoke to your own children as often as you spoke with your Prophets. I am only guessing what you want of me in this.'

****

'Where is Salmah? He should have returned by now. He is putting everything at risk.'

'Surely if God is with us, nothing Salmah can do will alter the outcome of our mission.' Deshaun challenged Joshua before realising the error of his words.

'Do not be so naïve Deshaun. There are forces at work here you know nothing about.'

'I do not understand.' Deshaun frowned and Joshua realised the young man really had no idea about the work of God. Joshua had been handed the role of helping God bring control over all the nations. Each nation had a choice, to give up their false gods in favour of the one true God or deal with the consequences.

Joshua understood why other nations may be confused, but there was growing dissent amongst his own people and he believed Salmah was at the heart of it. The leader of Judah was softening to the cause of the Canaanites and Joshua knew Salmah was struggling to reconcile the death of a nation, in favour of Israel.

Salmah did not understand the depths of God's power. Joshua himself could not be sure of God's plans, but he knew God wanted this victory for with it His power would reign forever.

'That is alright Deshaun. Bring the other leaders to me. I will explain God's plan. Salmah will have to be briefed later.' The old man patted the young soldier's shoulder as he spoke.

Chapter 11

'I have a really bad feeling about all of this Rahab. I wish there was more I could do.' Salmah sipped from his mug of ale as he sat across from the Priestess.

'You say your god will protect my family if I gather them before the invasion?'

'Our soldiers will have orders to leave your house alone. The leader of our people, Joshua, he believes God will bring down the walls and your home will be spared.'

'I am not sure I can accept that offer Salmah. I do not believe I can stand by and watch my neighbours perish, while I stay safely tucked away, hiding from the fighting.'

'But you must Rahab.' Salmah could hear the pleading in his own words.

The Priestess gently touched his hand where it rested on the table. The patrons had all departed shortly after the guards and Rahab had sent everyone home for the night. Salmah had hidden in her loft bed until she had locked the door behind Musaf. Now as they sat drinking ale and eating Musaf's legendary goat hotpot, Rahab could not help but feel the intensity of Salmah's words.

'Why do the people of Jericho have to perish at the hand of your God?'

The question came unexpectedly and Salmah could not think of an answer. He lowered his head for a moment, trying to find the right words to say. He believed in God, but he was not a preacher or prophet. The why of it all eluded him.

'I do not know Rahab. In truth, I do not understand it at all. I thought we were coming to Jericho to plead for asylum, a safe and prosperous place to raise the children of Israel. Now that I am here, I discover my leader wishes death to all your people. I cannot believe it is the wish of our God, for if it is, I no longer understand His will.'

'That makes two of us then.' Rahab smiled. 'You asked me what I do here. Do you still want to know?'

Salmah did not answer for a moment. In truth, he was afraid of what he would discover. There was a permanent place in his heart for Rahab now, yet he was the leader of the tribe of Judah and he was unsure of how his tribe would receive her when the walls fell. Finally, he nodded for Rahab to continue.

'When I was younger, I watched the women of Jericho. It did not take me long to realise I could never be one of them, not really: - to grow to an age of consent, to be married off to someone twice my age and bartered for, based on how much dowry my prospective husband could offer, in reality, to be sold to the highest bidder into marriage.' Rahab forced her rage down as she tried to keep her tone even.

Salmah stroked Rahab's hand as she spoke. 'So, you became a Priestess?'

'Yes. I was sixteen when I left my family home and established this Inn. I had been fighting with my family for two years, avoiding suiters and refusing to marry. I think they were happy to see the back of me in the end, although they had to forgo my dowry of course, but I have provided.' Rahab cupped Salmah's hand in hers and smiled.

'The Prince was one of my first customers. We had known each other as children and he took it upon himself to aid me in establishing my business.'

Rahab watched Salmah carefully. It had been a very long time since she had felt the flutter of butterflies in her stomach. Not since the day she had wrestled Uriah in the town square and forced him to apologise for picking a fight with her friend Tomos.

She had pinned him to the ground under her legs and sat on his chest heavily. As he had looked up at her, there had been fireworks exploding before her eyes. She was a few months short of her thirteenth birthdate and he was three years her senior.

'We had been *very* close childhood friends but as I came of marrying age, it became obvious to both of us that Hamilkot would never allow a union. I was never likely to be chosen to be the next Queen of

Jericho. Too poor a family, too head strong and too smart for a woman.'

'Did you love him?' Rahab nodded gently. 'Do you still love him?'

'No, that time is past. When I realised I could not marry the man I loved I decided to commit my life to Asherah. I think I was always destined to join the Goddess. I was never going to be like all the other girls. The call of nature was strong and my heart was never meant to be tied without love.'

Salmah hesitated before asking the question he had to ask. 'Can you put Asherah aside for Yahweh?'

'Do I have to? Rahab stood and moved from her side of the table to join Salmah. He swung around to straddle the bench-seat as Rahab stepped over his lap and lowered her face to his.

'I cannot marry you if…' Rahab covered Salmah's lips with hers and cupped his face in her hands as he placed his hands on her hips and pulled her to him.

****

Joshua allowed no misinterpretation as he explained to the tribal leaders how they were going to take the walls of Jericho. There were murmurs as the men of Israel quietly voiced their concerns. Joshua shared the vision God had given to him.

'You dragged my men and the men of Reuben away from our families to sit by and watch Priests and trumpets prance around the city walls putting on a show for the King of Jericho. How dare you waste our time like this Joshua?' The vein above the Gad leader's temple was pulsing as he spoke.

'I have done nothing Lavon except obey the word of our God.' Joshua tapped Nehushtan upon the ground for emphasis. The staff was renowned enough to have its own name. Lavon considered it for a moment. Nahushtan was a grand symbol of God's power. Its notoriety had spread amongst the Israelites when the Prophet had turned it into a snake before the Pharaoh of Egypt. Joshua's wielding of the symbol was not lost on the leader of Gad.

'You have been granted your lands and you will be free to return to them in short order.' Joshua continued.

As the questions died down, Joshua looked around for Salmah. He was still missing, yet to return from his visit with the whore. There was no written law to prevent unmarried men from fraternising with women of the night, but it was frowned upon and left a foul taste in the old man's mouth. Joshua shook his head with frustration.

'Deshaun, send Salmah to me as soon as he returns.' Joshua did not linger, he made his way to his tent to find a few moments of peace. He felt every one of his seventy-eight years and wondered over how long he had left on this earth.

Chapter 12

'Do you have to go?' Rahab rolled over onto her elbow and gently caressed Salmah's chest.

'Yes, I really should. Jacob is going to be angry enough.'

'Can I show you something first?' Rahab sat up and slipped her tunic on over her head. She tied it in place with a plum coloured cord.

'What do you want to show me?'

'You will have to come and see for yourself.' Rahab smiled mischievously and moved down the ladder from the loft bed and out of sight as Salmah busily pulled on his own clothing.

Rahab was waiting in the washroom below and handed Salmah a sweet cake as she ushered him out the door.

'Is it safe to go out on the street?' Salmah looked up and down the alley-way nervously.

'We will not be going far. Just stick to the shadows and we should be fine. If anyone comes by, you can always kiss me and pretend to be a client.'

Salmah winced but Rahab did not notice in the darkness. She took his hand and led him into the weaving walkways that took them behind the Inn and deeper into the city. It was only a few blocks of buildings before they found their destination.

A tall grove of trees obscured the moonlight above and the darkness only grew more impenetrable as Rahab guided Salmah deeper into the lush green forest that seemed so out of place amongst the harsh stone walls of the buildings nearby.

'Can you smell that?' Rahab asked as she pushed Salmah against a heavy bark covered trunk.

'All I can smell is you.'

'Then you should breathe a little deeper.' Rahab grinned. 'I come here when I feel I need to seek guidance from Asherah. Where do you go to speak to your god?'

'We receive the word of God from Joshua or occasionally the Priests.'

'Really? Your god does not speak directly to you?'

'No' Salmah frowned at the idea.

'Asherah speaks with visions and sometimes words into my mind. Oh, I wish you could hear her Salmah. Her words are like music and they are filled with love, not war.'

Rahab pulled Salmah by the hand away from the tree and towards what looked like a pool of water. The surface shimmered with the moonlight above and an unusual eerie light emanated from below the water. Salmah thought he could almost see beyond the surface but he lost the image as the Priestess pulled him past the pond.

Beyond on a raised dais of stone stood a collection of carved images. There was a woman holding a child against her body, but she had no arms. There were poles of timber trunks planted into the stone looking like lonely soldiers in the strange moonlight.

'What is that?' Salmah pointed to paintings on the wall beyond the poles.

'They are the stories of our ancestors; the legend of our faith.' Rahab bowed her head almost sadly.

'What is wrong?' The young man touched Rahab's hand and pulled her to his chest.

'My people have forgotten Asherah and the gods of Heaven. I can feel the Goddess's tears.' Rahab pulled Salmah closer to the wall. The images were difficult to see in the moonlight, but as the Priestess traced her hand along the paintings, Salmah began to see more clearly. 'This is Asherah and this is Moloch. It is said that they are brother and sister, but Asherah is not like Moloch. The Host of Heaven call him the Wayward Son.'

Salmah was quiet a moment. 'My people worshipped another god called Baal when they left Egypt but God was very angry about it. It is this lack of reverence for God that cost an entire generation entry to the Promised Land.'

'So, if they had not worshipped Baal, your people would have been here earlier? Thank your god for their mistake. If your father, or brother, or whoever it was had come all those years ago, we would never have met.'

'True enough. But they did make the mistake and here we are, ready to kill your people. Maybe if we had come earlier, Jericho might not have been so powerful and we might have been given sanctuary without a fight.'

'No, the timing would not have changed the hearts of powerful men. Your leader, Joshua is such a man and our King is no different and according to Asherah, Moloch is just the same.' Rahab lent her head on Salmah's shoulder and he wrapped his arm around her in response.

'Have you decided on our offer?'

'Our offer or yours?' Rahab challenged good naturedly.

'Both.'

'I will gather my family to the Inn when you give me the signal, we will all be ready.'

'That only answers one question.'

'True.' Rahab took Salmah's hand and gently ushered him out of the Goddesses grove. 'You must be on your way. The guards will change soon.'

****

Asherah knew meddling was forbidden. There were rules for the Host of Heaven but what was meddling and what was answering prayers? Yahweh had a habit of shifting the rules when she was not watching. Moloch meddled, of that she was sure.

After watching how Uriah had almost killed that poor girl at the Inn, Asherah could feel her frustration growing. Why did Yahweh let Moloch get away with such behaviour? It seemed only the good-natured gods obeyed the rules, while the worst offenders got away with whatever they wanted to. Asherah forced herself not to pout.

The Goddess pushed aside her annoyance at Moloch's disobedience and considered that when Yahweh finally decided to communicate with her once more she would have to discuss a suitable punishment for Moloch. In the mean-time she had her own work to do.

Asherah settled down on the soft crimson cushions that covered her marble divan. She loved her Sanctuary. From the grove of trees, to the gigantic waterfalls, to the flowing stream that rolled over rocks into a warm pool of effervescent water, it was her solitude, her place of relaxation and meditation.

Hidden above a thicket of trees, right in the middle of the township of Jericho, her home had remained invisible from prying eyes for decades. When the city had first been built it was small and her grove of trees had been large and central to the city. As the population had grown and the buildings swelled, the grove had been invaded by structures. Yet the sanctuary above remained undisturbed.

The Goddess relaxed and listened to her breathing as Rahab's thoughts came into her mind. Asherah was warmed by the woman's passion and waited for memories of Salmah to pass. It did not take long for Rahab's subconscious to begin mulling over her concerns. She was confused and torn between her commitment to her people and her growing feelings toward Salmah, but most of all she was confused about the Goddess.

Asherah waited and slowly opened Rahab's mind to the beauty of her oasis. As the Priestess's thoughts relaxed, Asherah released images into her mind. At first, she revealed a distant future, where the walls of a fortress were filled with women in white robes brandishing bows. There was so much she wanted to share with the young woman, but most of all, she wanted Rahab to know the people of Jericho would be protected.

Chapter 13

It was after midnight when Salmah made his way back into the camp. The young man had never set out to be a soldier and when Joshua had asked him to spy on the city of Jericho he had not thought for a moment he would fall in love with a Priestess of Asherah.

He could not help but wonder the fate of such a phenomenon. He was the leader of the tribe of Judah, one of the twelve tribes of Israel. How on earth was he to bring a follower of Ahserah into the fold of the One True God without repercussions?

His question did not linger for long. Deshaun heard him enter the tent they shared.

'Joshua wants to see you.'

'It is after midnight, I will see him in the morning.'

'He told me to send you to him as soon as you arrived back.

'He will not be awake Deshaun. He is nearly eighty for goodness sake. I will call on him at first light. I am tired.'

'I bet you are.'

Salmah ignored his friend's tone and rolled into his bed. He was not tired, he was elated and knew sleep would not be coming any time soon, but he had no desire to ruin his evening with another pointless debate with the old man.

'Do you want to hear Joshua's plan?' Deshaun spoke into the darkness.

Salmah considered pretending to be asleep, but he needed to know what was happening to ensure Rahab's safety.

'God's plan I am sure he called it.'

'You know him so well my friend. Those were his exact words.'

'No doubt.'

'The Priests will bring the victory, with God's power of course.' Salmah grunted but Dashaun continued excitedly. 'Can you believe they plan on bringing the walls down with trumpets and soldiers stomping feet?'

'No, I do not believe it.' God bringing down the walls on Jericho he already knew, but the method was news to him. He believed it; he simply did not understand it. 'What about all the people within, the smith, the baker, the tailors? It does not make sense Deshaun. Why would God want all those people to die? They have done nothing to hurt us, or to disrespect our beliefs or our God? It is their land! They have lived here for generations.'

Silence fell over the tent. Salmah heard Deshaun shift uncomfortably in his bedding. 'It is alright my friend. I do not expect you to know the answer.'

'You are worried about Rahab.' Deshaun sat up in the darkness and looked over to his friend, even though he knew he could not be seen.

'Yes and no. I am not cut out to be a soldier Deshaun. Killing people who have done nothing wrong makes little sense to me and that God would aid in such a mission, is even less comprehensible.'

'I am not much for understanding God Salmah but I understand a little of warfare. An army can only hope to win if they remain strong and appear invincible. As soon as the soldiers believe they might lose, they will flee back to their families.

We were starving in the dessert. We need the lands of the Canaanite people and there is fat chance they will share them willingly. If God shows his power, they will yield. Yes, some will die here, some of us will die too, but we have no other choice. To not fight, to not let God wield his power here and now is to guarantee the extinction of our people Salmah. Do you understand what that will mean!'

Salmah understood. Yet he did not feel comfortable. Before he had met Rahab, before she had shown him the temple of Asherah, before he had looked into her fiery eyes and seen her passion burning for her independence and her people he had been fine with God's plan. Now, he was not sure. He let the silence grow. 'I understand my friend but that does not mean I have to like it.'

****

Salmah awoke to the early grey morning light filtering through the thin fabric of his tent. His dreams had been frantic and filled with images of death. He could smell the soft musky scent of Rahab upon his tunic and the thought of her quickened his heart.

Joshua would be angry enough without any evidence of where he had been late into the previous evening. He stood and pulled his tunic off over his head, allowing the fragrance to linger for a moment. He quickly dressed in a fresh tunic and splashed his face with water before moving out into the first rays of sunlight rising from the east. The silhouette the sun cast of the walls of Jericho felt eerie in the dawn light. Salmah hurried to a meeting he had no desire to experience but knew was inevitable.

Joshua was wide awake and already rummaging through reports. A platter of dates and cheese remained untouched on the low table, almost hidden below hand-painted goat skin maps and scrolls scribed in the man's own hand.

The old man looked up with tired eyes as Salmah entered. 'Ah, I see you have finally found the time to join us Salmah. Is it just me, or do the men of Judah hold all those in leadership with such contempt?' Joshua barely glanced up from his work. Salmah chose to ignore the goading.

'You are busy early Sir.' Joshua waved a hand for Salmah to take a seat on the cushions opposite him, but did not look up. 'You asked for me.'

The silence grew between the two men. Salmah waited, keeping his frustration hidden, while Joshua seemed to continue to ignore the young man with great purpose.

Salmah looked at the scrolls of information and the maps and tried to make up his mind if they were relevant to this campaign or another sacking of another innocent city somewhere else in the Canaanite lands.

A few minutes passed before Joshua pushed aside his maps and focussed once more on Salmah. He cleared the low table of notes and found the platter of food hidden below. 'Hungry?' Joshua pushed the platter closer to Salmah's side.

'Not as hungry as I have been, but getting very close.' The younger man smiled and Joshua returned the grin.

'You are not happy Salmah, that is obvious.' Joshua did not wait for an answer. 'I share your concerns, possibly not as fervently as you do, but believe me I can appreciate your stance in this matter. I am older and have lost much of my vigour for lost causes many years ago. I have seen my friends cast out of the Promised Land. I have waited forty years for this time to come to pass and any delays serve only to aggravate me, which I am sure you can appreciate.'

Salmah was not sure if he should speak, or only nod. The choice was taken from him as Joshua continued. 'I will send a messenger to give the King of Jericho a chance. You will be that messenger.'

Salmah was shocked at such an opportunity. To be able to give the people of Jericho a choice and to see Rahab once more before the city fell was a blessing. He prayed the men of Jericho were not so proud that they would not yield, but deep down he was not optimistic. 'Do you think it will make a difference?'

'To those in Jericho, possibly, possibly not, but God has told me it is important to the Israelites. For our peace and prosperity, we need a unified front. I have no use for a rift between us. The walls will fall and I am sure Deshaun has briefed you by now, on how that is to pass, but at least the people will not be on the walls and if they surrender without incident, then they will live. We can do no more than that.'

'Getting to the King might prove difficult.'

'I am sure your *friend* will be able to make the arrangements.' Salmah smiled at the emphasis and almost spoke his mind on the matter. Instead he let the comment go.

'I will speak with Rahab. How long do I have?'

'Two days. Then we will begin the ritual. On the first day, we will march the Ark of our Lord with all our men around the walls of Jericho once. It is up to you to impart the truth of my words on the King of Jericho. If they have not taken our Lord seriously by then, they soon will. When the ground begins to rumble beneath their feet, they will know the power of the One True God. He has promised to deliver Jericho into our hands on the seventh day after the ritual begins.

Salmah breathed a sigh of relief. He believed Joshua with all his heart and mind. If God had told him the walls would fall, then fall they would. At least now he had almost nine days to see how he and Rahab might save the people of Jericho.

Chapter 14

Asherah felt the presence of Moloch before she heard his voice. Her skin tingled with the discomfort that always accompanied his visits. 'Sister, so good to see you.'

'How many times have I told you not to call me that!'

'I have lost count *Sister*.' Moloch bowed before Asherah without reverence, ignoring her tone.

'Are you lying in wait for more sacrifices?' Asherah hated goading her brother, yet it was almost impossible not to speak her mind when he was around.

'There is never any shortage of children being offered up to me *Asherah*, you know the people are beyond saving.'

'Not all of us live to feed off their suffering Moloch. Yahweh has this place under his control. Why are you here?' Asherah smoothed her dress as she floated above the walls of Jericho, unseen by the innocents below.

She had risen from her oasis to watch the sun rise over her temple and now as she looked at the walls of Jericho her heart ached for the lives that would be lost over this event and her spirit yearned for Yahweh to find another way.

'Most of us do. The people of this world do not appreciate the lives they are given. They feed my power with every word and every deed. See over there.' Moloch pointed to an alley way a short walk from Rahab's Inn. Upon the rough cobble stones in full view lay the body of a young woman who could not be a day over fourteen. Her dress was torn and her body covered in blood. As they watched, early rising residents passed by without stopping or taking a second look. 'A perfect example.' Moloch laughed.

Asherah closed her eyes and tried to block out the mocking words of her brother. She reached out with her spirit, seeking the girl's essence. It had departed hours earlier. 'She is in heaven now.'

'Yes, yes. Between you and Yahweh, they all make it to heaven eventually but they make such a mess of this life it is a constant source of entertainment.'

'They deserve life and you should be the one never to see the light of day. You goad them, you tempt them, you feed their weak minds. It is your fault, not theirs.'

'Oh Sister, you know that they have a choice. Father made sure of that. They have been making poor choices since the dawn of time and they will continue to do so into the future. I am yet to understand why you both do not wipe the world clean and start over. Seriously! Or better still, bring them all into Heaven now, give them the promise of eternal life now and be done with the experiment.'

'It is not an experiment you oaf. You really do not get it do you.' Moloch frowned. 'Yahweh wants heaven to be on this world. Humanity is not equipped to live forever, not yet. We get bored with it, how much more so would they in their current form? They are yet to evolve into a state that lives forever and only time and the Grace of Yahweh yet to come, can hope to achieve their maturity.'

'I am bored with this. You are so naive. They will never change, not in a million years. I will continue to draw on those who will worship me for eternity.' Moloch smiled gleefully and disappeared into the mist of the morning clouds.

'Oh that is it, run away from the debate. You always do that when you are not winning.' Asherah almost screamed into the sky as the sun finally cleared the horizon. The warmth it delivered soaked into her spirit and she could feel Yahweh's love envelop her. 'He will never understand.' The Goddess spoke softly to the sun as though it understood.

****

Salmah had only a few more minutes to make the long climb to Rahab's window. Her Inn was on the western side of the city and the morning light had not yet reached the horizon. The grey pre-dawn light gave the young Israelite just enough time to scale the rope before the sun crested the hills beyond. Frantically he pulled the rope into the window. As he turned, he nearly bumped into the Priestess descending the ladder from her loft.

She stepped into his personal space, her naked light brown skin glistening in the dim light. 'I was not expecting your return so soon.' Rahab grinned mischievously as she stroked Salmah's chest.

'We have nine days.' Salmah drew Rahab into his arms. She rubbed her body against him as they kissed.

'A shame I have an Inn to open.' The Priestess rubbed her hips against Salmah's one last time before she pulled away.

Salmah cleared his throat knowing his voice would fail him if he spoke. He took in her beauty once more before speaking. 'And I have plans to discuss with you. You are a constant distraction woman. No wonder God calls his Priests to chastity. There would never be a prayer to God or vision interpreted if not.

Rahab laughed as she reached for her tunic. As she pulled it on over her head Salmah stepped in and stopped her, holding her arms up, he pushed the tunic away from her face and kissed her. Then his lips travelled down her body gently kissing her neck and beyond.

'Oh, who cares about work, the staff will not be here for another hour.' Rahab tossed the tunic to the floor and leapt into Salmah's arms, wrapping her bare legs around his body.

****

'How do you believe I am going to get you into the palace? What part of no visitors are you having difficulty understanding?' Danal put her hands on her hips for added effect.

'Yes, but if anyone can convince Uriah's personal guard, or maybe his brothers to allow me an audience it is you.' Danal had been Rahab's closest friend when they were children, except Danal was noble born and Rahab was something entirely different.

Danal was in fact the most likely to be betrothed to Uriah although he had managed to avoid any such engagement for more years than Rahab had thought possible. His father was getting older and he was the heir. It was only a matter of time before he was forced to marry.

'You are unbelievable. You want me to help you smuggle a spy into the palace?

'Danal, you know me. Since when have I ever done anything to hurt anyone?'

'Do you really want me to answer that?' Danal pouted.

'Alright, when have I ever intentionally hurt anyone who was not already hurting me?' Danal knew Rahab could look after herself. She had been one of the girls who fought the boys when they were children. Yet she was also the first to stand in the place of anyone who was too weak or too afraid to look after themselves. If there was a fight to be had to protect anyone, Danal knew Rahab would be there.

'I get it Rahab. I will see what I can arrange, but like I said, the palace is locked up tighter than a drum. Something is not right. Uriah has not been out publicly….'

The sound of trumpets reached the young women. Both looked questioningly at each other.

Rahab turned and began taking the steps to the top of the battlements above the Inn two at a time. Her legs were long and fit, Danal followed.

'What is that all about?' Danal reached the top a few moments behind Rahab. 'Oh, my goodness.'

Below the walls of Jericho, the Israelites had begun to march around the city. Rahab strained to see the people below. There was a small group of men in flowing robes and they were carrying a large gilded box upon long poles. The trumpets were being blown behind them and hundreds of men were joining the procession. It was the strangest sight the Priestess had ever seen, almost amusing if she had not known the exhibition was meant to unnerve the city occupants.

The trumpets were loud and their tune sounded up and over the walls like thunder, but there was something almost serene about the pace. Calm, calculated and methodical, it set a somewhat sombre mood amongst the men gathered on the walls.

'That is the first time I have seen Uriah outside since the Israelites arrived.' Danal pointed to the wall in front of the Palace. Uriah shielded his eyes as he gauged the forces below. They carried spears and blades, but none was drawn. They were simply marching around the walls.

People scrambled up the stairs all around the city perimeter to get a glimpse of the procession. The older and less agile called out from the city streets, asking questions about the cause of the noise. Some lost interest and returned to their market stalls or other duties, while many took their place in line, hoping to discover more of what was happening.

By the time the head of the snake of men reached all the way around the city walls, the tail was only just leaving. Rahab was no expert but there must have been thousands of soldiers, all fit and healthy and ready to fight. The sight was both glorious and unnerving.

'Get me that meeting Danal, there is a lot riding on this. I have somewhere to be.' Rahab turned around and descended the stairs. Salmah was standing at the window looking at the horde below when she entered the back room of the Inn.

'So, it begins. Seven days and counting.'
Salmah announced without taking his eyes from his
people. There was no joy in his words, no hint of
honour or pride. Finally, he moved his gaze to Rahab.
'I am sorry.'

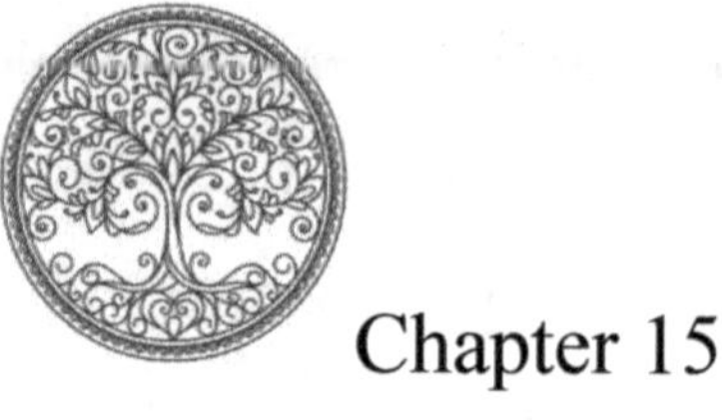# Chapter 15

Uriah held his father's hand. His brothers had departed only moments before. The argument over the Israelite forces camped beyond their walls had raged and Uriah had used all his diplomacy to keep a semblance of peace.

Hamilkot looked healthy. His colour was good, his heart strong. The physicians puzzled over his condition. A daily ritual of bathing had been established and Uriah could not help but smile. His father would have found great enjoyment in such a practice if he had been conscious. The young women used warmed water in buckets and sponged the King's body from top to bottom. They changed the bedding and his clothing daily.

Uriah lifted the potion from the side table and peered into the vial. It was a milky liquid that smelt benign and the Prince wondered if it was wise to administer the concoction. His father was unconscious for no apparent reason and poison had not been ruled out, Yet he trusted Malic. He was the King's Chief Physician and had been with him since they were boys.

The old healer claimed the potion was Milk Thistle and would cleanse the King's liver from any toxins should he have been poisoned. If nothing else, he was adamant it would keep the King in good health until he awoke.

Uriah lifted his father's head and gently drizzled the liquid into the King's mouth. The swallowing reflex was not present and Malic had warned Uriah to take the process slowly or risk choking his father.

The doors pushed open without warning and Uriah juggled the vial precariously. 'What on earth are you doing?' Uriah growled at the intruder as he gained control of the potion and gently lowered his father's head to the cushion.

'My apology your Grace. You have an unexpected and rather urgent visitor?'

Uriah looked from the vial still in his hand and the guard at the door. 'Fetch Malic. Have him meet me in the King's Hall.'

The guard bowed as the Prince moved to the doorway. 'Who?' Uriah asked almost as an afterthought.

'The Innkeeper your Grace and it appears she has brought an Israelite into the Palace.'

Uriah took a deep breath, forcing his anger down. He did not wish a repeat of the other night. How on earth had he nearly allowed his Captain of the Guard to kill that poor girl? He knew his rage was unprovoked, yet deep down he felt a betrayal he could not fully explain.

The long walk through the Palace to the King's Hall gave the Prince time to consider Rahab. There had been a time when they were younger that he had honestly thought they would marry but as he reached maturity, his father began making other arrangements to join his family to one of the wealthier houses in Jericho. Uriah was the oldest son and as such could never hope to marry for love.

He could hardly take this misfortune out on Rahab. She had not rejected him, it was his family who had been unwilling to accept her and now that she was a Priestess of Asherah, they never would.

She was a woman of means now, wealthy beyond many of the great houses of Jericho, but she was tainted by a reputation that could never be expunged. It made little sense to the Prince. He was within his rights to frequent her establishment and take whomever he chose to his bed and still maintain his place of honour amongst royalty, but as an independent and unmarried woman, Rahab would never be considered for marriage into the Royal Household.

As the Prince approached the Hall, his guards opened the heavy dark wooded doors which groaned under their own weight. Uriah took a deep breath, knowing the sight of Rahab was always difficult. He had stopped taking her to his bed years before. When Rahab had left home and opened her Inn, they had perpetuated their relationship at first, but eventually Rahab had replaced herself with one of her

Priestesses. He could still remember her words, *we can never have each other Uriah and I will not be a King's Mistress.*

The doors opened as the Prince made his final few steps to the King's Hall. Prepared as he was, the sight of Rahab still took his breath away.

'Your Grace,' Rahab curtsied 'I apologise for the intrusion. Will the King not be joining us?'

'The King is otherwise occupied and I am busy so, to what do we owe this unexpected visit?' Uriah knew he was being curt, but he needed to keep the meeting formal, especially in the presence of the Israelite.

'I am sorry to disturb you Prince.' Salmah bowed.

'I do not recall asking for you to speak.' Uriah scowled at Salmah and the two men stared at one another for a moment.

Rahab touched Salmah's chest much as she had stopped Uriah at her Inn, but with less emphasis. 'Your Grace. Salmah is here as an envoy of the Israelites.

'Since when do you broker meetings with our enemies Rahab? I knew you were involved, but this!' Uriah opened his hand toward the spy and frowned.

'By this do you mean trying to save the people of Jericho and maintain some peace and order? I am a Priestess of Asherah *Your Grace*, it is my duty.' Rahab kept her tone calm, but her features betrayed her agitation. Uriah knew that look and smiled, breaking the tension.

'I have been rude. I apologise Priestess. Come.' Uriah waved them both to a raised platform of soft cushions and a small marble table. The meeting area sat to the left of the throne upon a wooden floor, surrounded by potted palms with two long steps carved out of sandstone leading upward.

Rahab lowered herself to the cushions and nodded her head for Salmah to join her. The leader of Judah took off his sandals and crossed his legs as he sat. There were ornate carvings all over the solid stone walls of the hall like nothing the young man had ever seen.

There had been talk of grand statues and carvings from Joshua and some of the men who had travelled from Egypt all those years ago, but Salmah had never seen anything like it with his own eyes. The shrine of the Goddess had been beautiful, but the King's Hall was simply majestic.

'Refreshments for my guests.' Uriah commanded and servants scurried in with clay cups, a large jug of watered wine, platters of food and soft moistened cloths for the guests to wipe their hands with.

The Prince waited for the servants to leave the platform and spoke quietly. 'What do you propose Rahab?'

'I believe it best if Salmah explains. I do not know and have not seen the power of his God.'

Salmah nodded. 'Joshua, the leader of my people claims God will bring down the walls of your city in seven days of the ritual march you witnessed this morning, if you have not surrendered Jericho to our Lord.' Uriah could feel the growl growing in his throat.

'Maybe I should have explained after all.' Rahab smiled to break the tension. 'You have to understand these men have wandered the desert for forty years. Diplomacy is not Salmah's strongest trait. I think maybe he should have lead with the fact he is here to hopefully save the lives of those in Jericho.'

'Of course. I am sorry. Rahab can attest that I am not very savvy on negotiations. The sad fact is I am probably the best of all the tribes.' Uriah laughed at Salmah's declaration.

'I have spent my life learning how to negotiate with Kings and Princes. I have to say I have never had to negotiate with a god before.' Uriah took a sip from his cup and placed it on the table.

'Asherah promised me in a dream that the people of Jericho would be safe Uriah. Then Salmah came to me with his news.'

'And how did Salmah know how to find you and even more importantly how did he get inside the city walls?' Uriah's tone was even and unchallenging but Rahab could see the feeling behind his eyes.

'I would never betray the people of Jericho Uriah, no more than I could betray anyone, of any nation. Asherah is the goddess of nature, love, birth; not death.'

'So, what does this Joshua want of me? To just lay down my father's city and open the gates?'

'That would be a nice gesture, but I do not believe it is that easy.' Salmah frowned as he spoke. He had been thinking deeply about the situation and had come to understand that the walls of Jericho would fall no matter what the outcome of this meeting.

'Then what do you suggest?' Uriah took a handful of nuts and threw them into his mouth one at a time. The action seemed relaxed to the untrained eye but Rahab knew the Prince well enough to know he was agitated.

'Get your men to leave the walls. If they are on the battlements when the walls fall hundreds, possibly thousands will die. Ensure that anyone who resides as Rahab does in or near the walls is evacuated.

Joshua does not want the death of all the inhabitants of Jericho, he wants them to fall before the God of Israel.' Uriah scoffed and Salmah put up his hand. 'I understand, really I do. I wonder about Joshua's motive myself, but there is no doubt that the God of our people is with him. We crossed the Jordan with all our possessions. If I had not seen it with my own eyes, I would not have believed it either.'

'I saw it.' Uriah interrupted. 'I know the power you speak of, but my father is not indisposed. He is unconscious and has been for days.' Rahab gasped and there was a moment of uncomfortable silence.

'Uriah, I am so sorry. What do the physicians say?' Rahab touched the Prince's hand gently provoking one of the guards to draw his sword.

Uriah held up his hand. 'Where is Malic, find the Physician. Now!' The Prince growled at the guard with his sword still drawn, realising Malic had still not arrived. 'Leave us.'

'Is that wise your Grace?' Uriah answered the guard's question with a sneer that made Salmah smile.

'If I take my men from the walls and my father recovers he will kill me. If I take the men from the walls and the King does not recover, the royal family will lose support from the commanders of the army and the King's council.'

'If you do not bring your people down from the walls they will die. The city will fall in less than six days now. Regardless of what you choose to do, is it not better to save as many lives as possible?'

'I will think on what you propose.' Uriah remained silent a moment. 'You know I do not believe in any of the gods, well I did not a week ago. When I witnessed your people cross the Jordan I questioned my lack of belief for the first time in my life. We had been raised to encourage the population to follow the gods for it kept them appeased, but our own lessons as children were of strategy, politics and innovation. It seems they are useless against the gods.'

'Asherah will deliver you into safety Uriah. She told me so.'

The doors to the Hall opened once more and Malic entered, his robes shining with silver and lavender thread. The Physician eyed Rahab suspiciously and the hair on the Priestess's neck rose in answer to his stare.

'You called your Grace.' Malic bowed deeply, grandly swishing his robe with his right hand.

'Where have you been? I was interrupted and I need you to continue with father's draft.' The physician looked from Rahab to Uriah with wide eyes, as though a great secret had been exposed.

'I apologise your Grace. I was detained. I will see to it immediately.' Malic turned quickly and almost scurried from the room.

'Is Malic your father's physician?' Rahab raised an eyebrow.

'Yes, he has been with father since they were boys. He always cares for the King. Why?'

Rahab knew Malic but there was something not quite right about him today. 'It is probably nothing.'

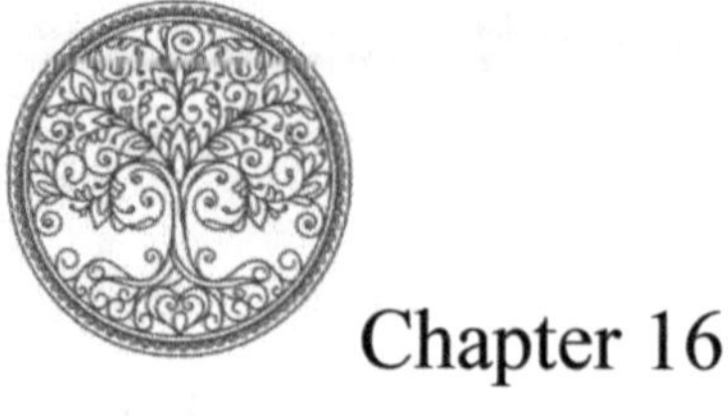

Chapter 16

Malic left for the King's apartment swallowing the nervous saliva rising in his throat. When the Prince had asked him why he was late, he honestly could not remember. He had not even heard the first guard call for his attendance.

One moment he had been in his quarters making a new thistle potion for the King and the next a guard was rapping on his door, grumbling he was late to the Hall. When he looked down at his hands he saw he had accidentally poured mandrake into the thistle potion. What a stupid error, it could have killed the King. Why on earth had he been so careless?

Malic rushed to the King's quarters. He opened the door and walked to Hamilkot's bedside. The King looked well. He picked up the vial the Prince had used earlier and smelt the contents. They seemed fine. Malic felt the King's pulse, the heartbeat was slow and strong, just as it should be.

The Physician wiped the beads of sweat from his brow and checked the potion once more. He tapped his little finger gently on the rim and tasted the liquid. It was untainted. Relief flooded Malic's mind.

He could tell no-one of what had happened, they would think him mad. Instead he would ensure that another physician made the potion under his supervision. Maybe his age was getting the better of him. There were those who succumbed to memory loss. He hoped the aging disease had not come to him early.

Satisfied, the Physician left the King's apartment, closing the doors carefully. As he did so he felt a coolness to the air. It seemed winter was coming early this year.

****

'What do you think he will do?' Salmah helped Rahab clear the tables as Musaf closed the door behind himself and left for the night.

'I have no idea Salmah, what would you do? He is doomed either way. His brothers want to fight your people now. It is only the logistics of a closed city stopping them. If his father were awake, Hamilkot would have been razing your encampment already. Uriah never had the heart for fighting. Diplomacy and scholarly pursuits yes, fighting, no.'

'You love him?'

Rahab looked up at Salmah and could see fear in his eyes for the first time. 'No, I loved him, a long time ago.'

'Will you leave with me once the city falls?'

'That depends.'

'On what?'

'On Joshua I expect.' Salmah knew Rahab was right. If Joshua would not allow Rahab to come with him into the lands of the Canaanite, then he would travel no further.

'He will welcome you. You have served the god of our people.'

'I have served Asherah.'

'Their causes are aligned it seems. Let us not debate the gods tonight. I will have to return to Joshua soon.' Salmah pulled the Priestess to him.

'I thought we still had six days left.'

'Maybe, maybe not. Let us not worry about tomorrow.' Salmah gently lifted Rahab onto the closest table and kissed her. She dropped the half empty mugs of ale she held to the ground and pushed the tin plates to the floor. They both laughed at the sudden noise.

Salmah's worries over Rahab's acceptance into his tribe and the war of the gods were pushed aside as Rahab kissed his lips passionately and rushed to lift her skirt up to her thighs.

****

'I have no idea why father made you heir.' Uriah's brothers were gathered and Adon was taking charge as he always did. A big man with broad shoulders and an angry scar on his face, he presented a formidable figure.

'I think it has something to do with his age.' Ikidran quipped, raising his jug of ale and swaying with the effort.

'Oh shut up Iki. You are drunk again.' Adon frowned at his youngest brother.

'No, not even close.' Iki grinned. 'Uriah is the wisest and oldest. That is why he is in charge.'

'I am right here!' Uriah pointed to his own chest.

'We have to fight Uriah. If we stand by and let them prance around goading us, it will be humiliating.'

'Better a little humiliation than annihilation.' Iki poured more ale into his mug, swaying all the while.

'Father would fight. You know he would.' The heat was rising to Adon's cheeks and the vein on his temple was pulsing erratically.

'Yes, he would.' Uriah spoke quietly. 'But father is unconscious and no matter what you believe brother, the gods have put me in charge. I do not like it any more than you do, but it is as they indented.

'Since when have you become religious?' Adon poked Uriah firmly in the chest.

'Since I witnessed the waters of the Jordan stop and that horde crossed without the loss of one man.

The Prince waved his hand toward the balcony which overlooked the Israeli camp.

'I will drink to that.' Iki saluted.

'What are you talking about? They are men, just men.' Adon scowled in Iki's direction.

'Yes, men who disappeared into the desert forty years ago and have not been seen or heard of since and now here they are, to claim their *Promised Land* just as the stories claimed they would.' Uriah stared challengingly at his brother.

'So, you are just going to hand it to them, just like that! What happens to us all when they invade? Do you really believe that we just walk away? Do you think they will let us live out of the kindness of their hearts?'

'The Israelite claims we have six more days before the walls fall. Let us see what transpires. If what they claim is true, their god will show his hand and then maybe you will understand what I have already seen. If not, we can use that time to plan an assault. If we open the gates, they will pour in. If we descend the walls to attack, they will pick us off like sparrows. We need to be strategic. No one does anything without my order, you understand Adon?'

Iki slapped his bigger brother on the back. 'He gets it Uriah. He might have the thickest head of us all, but he gets it. Say yes Adon.' Iki nodded slowly as if talking to an imbecile.

Adon glared avoiding the temptation to thump his brother, his dark eyebrows forming one big crease on his forehead as he considered Uriah's request. 'I make no promises. Father would have already mounted the walls and killed as many of the bastards as he could by now.'

'Yes, true and he would have died with all the men he sent into the charge.' Uriah shook his head. He knew his words were falling on deaf ears.

'Better to die trying than sit here and await execution.' Adon stormed out of Uriah's apartment, slamming the heavy wooden door with extreme prejudice. An ornate vase balanced on a pedestal by the doorway crashed to the floor.

'Keep an eye on him Iki.'

'Of course brother.' Iki made to leave, then hesitated, looking over his shoulder at his oldest brother. 'Do you mind if I call on Danal. You know, being the end of days and all?' Iki grinned mischievously.

'If she will have you brother, why not?'

'Just checking, you are in line for the King's job, I guessed you would be marrying her soon.'

'If we live through this, I will abdicate Iki. There was only ever one woman I wanted for my wife and if we live through this, I will give up the throne to marry her.'

Iki gave Uriah a sympathetic look. 'You should drink more.' He smiled. 'See you in the morning. Hopefully Adon is in a better mood by then.'

'Good night Iki, sleep well.'

Chapter 17

Adon wandered down to the market square below the Palace. The people were oblivious to the dangers that awaited them in the coming days and the Prince was angry with them, with his brothers and even with his father for being bed-ridden at such an important time.

The smell of roasting meat filled his nostrils and the big man pushed his way through the throng of people to find the source. It did not take him long to sniff out the sizzling lamb that rolled slowly above the burning coals, spitting fat into the night air one delicious drop at a time.

Men were lined up to buy the flat bread and spiced meat but Adon knew he only had to push up to the front to be served immediately. Instead he waited his turn, allowing the scent to bring peace to his soul.

Food always provided serenity for the big man, the reason he was a big man he knew, but whoring like Iki had never really appeased his senses. Fighting on the other hand often drowned out the grumbling of his stomach and it remained the only possible activity that could draw his mind from food. Well today there was to be no fighting, so the lingering smell of crispy skinned lamb would have to suffice.

Adon was nearly to the head of the line when Nimal recognised him. 'Your Grace, you should have said, here take mine, I will wait for another.'

'No need Nimal. I am happy to wait my turn. Half the pleasure of eating is in the waiting.' The big man grinned at the Captain of the guard.

'Well at least come and join me and the men for an ale or two before you leave Sire.'

Adon nodded as Nimal pointed to a long table under a stretched-out sail made of animal skins. The cover provided protection from the weather, but there would be no rain tonight. The sky was clear and filled with the twinkling of stars. There were a dozen men or more, filling their bellies with food and ale while a handful of street whores and beggar boys hovered nearby hoping for some favour.

Adon asked for two servings and tipped the cook an extra copper coin. The man nodded his gratitude and carried on serving, while the Prince made his way to the long table to find a space near Nimal and a jug of ale brimming with froth awaiting him.

'Hell of a day Sire!' Nimal spoke with his mouth full. Adon was not offended; on the contrary, he hated the stuffiness of royal life, with lessons in etiquette and table manners.

Uriah had always relished the challenge and fought to impress the visiting dignitaries who graced the halls of Jericho from time to time, but not Adon, he hated the pompous costumes, the hoity-toity manners and horse dung politeness of those meetings.

No-one ever said what they were really thinking, no they were all just two-faced liars saying one thing and doing something totally opposite when it suited them, hoping never to get caught out.

'You can say that again Nimal. What do you make of those Israeli twits?'

'Not sure what they are thinking Sire. What's with the parade? They hoping to deafen us into giving up?' Nimal laughed and his men tried hard to make the Captain feel like his joke was funny. An awkward silence followed before Adon answered.

'My brother is considering it.' Adon knew he was speaking out of turn, but he was simmering with frustration.

'He can't be Sire! What is he thinking? Canaanites don't give up for anyone, never have, never will. What does your father have to say?'

Adon knew he had said too much in that moment. His father's condition remained a secret. 'He does not agree of course.' He lied.

'Oh, thank the Goddess if you believe in that kind of stuff Sire. What is the plan then?'

Adon's mind was racing. He felt like a rabbit in the sights of an arrow with attack the only option. He took another mouthful to give him time to compose himself. 'I am working on a plan. How many men can you muster within three days?'

'Well Sir, that is short notice, but the town guard will do as I say. What of the army?'

'The army offers no support at this time. The King, Uriah and all of the King's Council remain undecided. We should prepare for the worst. If they fail to act before the Israelites decide to breech the walls, we will mount an attack of our own.'

'But how Sire, we can't open the gates.' Nimal spoke in a low whisper now, concerned someone might hear and pass on the information to the King or even Uriah. He knew the oldest Prince was no warrior, but he was clever, still skilled with a sword and not one to double-cross.

'I have an idea for that Nimal. That is why I need the extra few days. Gather your men quietly, let them know the assault will be at night and they should be ready in three days. Tell them if any word leaks out, it will be me they must answer to.' Adon skulled his ale and ripped a mouthful of lamb roll into his mouth, chewing unceremoniously, the food visibly over-gorging his mouth as it had for Nimal earlier.

 Chapter 18

Salmah held Rahab against his bare chest, her eyes were closed and her breathing deep. The morning gloom was giving way to sunrise and Salmah closed his eyes in silent prayer. *It has been forty years since you promised us this land Lord, but do we really have to take it from others? Is there not another way?*

'What are you thinking?' Rahab spoke quietly into the dimness of their loft bedroom.

'I was asking God for another way.'

Rahab remained silent a moment. 'Does your God really want my people to die so that his can prosper?'

'Joshua believes He does.'

'What do you believe Salmah?'

'I believe we should all be able to live in this land peacefully.'

'That is not the way of men though is it. They wish to possess everything all for themselves. The

very thought of sharing is impossible to comprehend.'
Rahab waited, gauging if now was the right time to
speak the truth.

'Just take me for instance. The men of this city
either want me married off, therefore owned by a man
to do with what he wants, or they consider me
damaged and unworthy. Men like to own things, to
control everything. The idea that I would choose not
to be with a man has been impossible for them to
fathom.'

Salmah thought about Rahab's words. He knew
she was speaking of more than men not sharing their
land with his people. 'Is this your way of saying you
will not marry and leave with me?'

'It is my way of saying men will never agree to
share or compromise on what they want. Joshua will
allow me to live. He will honour the agreement he
struck with you, but he is no better than any other man
Salmah. He will not accept that I chose not to be
owned by a man.'

'I will not give him the choice Rahab. When we
leave Jericho after this battle, my tribe will be granted

lands beyond Joshua's influence and I *will* take you as my wife if you so *choose*.'

Rahab lifted her head and moved toward Salmah's lips with hers. 'And what if I do not ….' The trumpets sounded beyond the walls and Rahab jumped with fright. 'Here we go again.' She rolled onto her back and sighed.

Salmah threw aside the covers and pulled on his tunic before climbing down the ladder to the cook room below. He watched the fighting men of the twelve tribes follow the Priests as a repeat of the procession from the day before.

The goal was obviously to bring the people of Jericho into a place of fear and trepidation. Today the procession grew louder and the walls of the city shook with the growing intensity of the vibration that emanated from the marching feet and blasting trumpets. Salmah could see the show of force was doing what was intended.

Rahab joined the young leader of Judah and wrapped her arms around his waist, laying her face against his back. 'You have to go.'

'You are so clever Rahab. Yes I must return to Joshua. It has been days and there is no word from the Palace and I need to keep him informed. I will leave after dark.'

Rahab tried not to think of Salmah leaving her for any length of time. She could not remember ever feeling so vulnerable before meeting him. It was as though he had sucked the courage from her bones the very moment they had first met.

It was more than their alliance that kept her thinking of him. He was caring, unlike any man she had ever met; more willing to sacrifice himself for the needs of others, for her.

Rahab pushed the melancholy aside. 'Help me get ready to open this morning. After the staff are here, we will take another walk.'

Salmah turned and embraced Rahab. She kissed his cheek gently, took his hand and walked him out into the dining area.

****

It was midday before Rahab managed to escape the Inn, leaving her staff to tend to the regulars and visitors alike. She needed time with Asherah and she hoped Salmah would join her in prayer. For them to continue to be lovers into the future, he had to understand she could not abandon the Goddess.

'Where are we going?' Salmah became apprehensive.

'You will see.' Rahab smiled as she took Salmah's hand. He pulled away reflexively; an outward show of affection was dangerous.

Rahab was undeterred, she reached out and took his hand again, patting it with her other hand reassuringly.

'Are you not afraid someone might see us?'

'What will they do? Uriah already knows you are in the city. Yes, scaling the walls in full view would not be a good idea, but no one here in the street knows who you are Salmah.' Rahab emphasized her point with a broad wave of her hand toward the milling crowds.

She was right. The market square was alive with activity. Fabric merchants with long lengths of beautiful coloured cloth bartered over prices. The smell of freshly roasting meat and baked bread wafted through the streets and alleys as they continued their walk.

An old lady with a tray covered in polished stones affixed to bands of leather pushed her way forward. 'A gift for your lady good Sir.'

'Another time.' Rahab smiled and the old woman moved on, recovering quickly and hawking her wares to the next face she saw. 'See, no one cares Salmah. An army is camped outside the city walls but commerce goes on unencumbered, as though tomorrow will look after itself.'

It did not take long for the grove of trees to come into view. Salmah had thought they were heading towards the temple but he could not be sure. It had been dark last time they visited. 'You have shown me your temple Rahab. Why are we returning?'

'I need you to meet someone.'

Salmah felt uncomfortable for the first time since meeting Rahab. 'Who?'

'You will see.'

Salmah pulled on Rahab's hand to bring her to a halt. 'You keep saying that. The only reason people say that is if they are unwilling to explain themselves.'

Rahab stepped forward and wrapped one hand around Salmah's face, stroking his cheek with her thumb. 'You asked me if I could join you after this siege is over. You recall?' Salmah nodded, feeling Rahab's breath upon his face. 'You need to trust me and you need to accept me as I am or that can never happen. Please, trust me now.'

Salmah brought Rahab's hand to his face and kissed it. He knew what she wanted now and he struggled with the choice. God had already punished his people for worshipping other gods. Joshua would disown him, he would be cast out of his tribe and rejected if he consorted with the Goddess, but he loved Rahab. He could only hope that God understood that his acceptance of Rahab did not change his faith in the One True God.

'I will join you. But if God strikes me down it is your fault, just you remember that' Rahab frowned until Salmah grinned mischievously.

She slapped him on the arm with the flat of her hand playfully. 'You know that is a terrible thing to say.'

Chapter 19

Iki followed Adon into the market place as he had for the past few days. His brother was never far away from food; Adon was stubborn and awkward and at times a little stupid but always hungry. He was a skilled warrior without a doubt but not a tactician and never likely to be commander material, yet Uriah had asked him to keep an eye on the warrior Prince, so Iki had done so.

He took his seat in the tavern across the street from where Adon now sat. He could smell the spirits drift from the bar making his palms sweat with the thought of the amber liquid running down his throat.

'What can I get you Sir?' The same pretty young barmaid had been attending him each day and today she smiled patiently as she waited to take his order.

Iki was tempted, so tempted. There were two vices he knew he struggled with, drink and women and both of them stood just within his reach but this was Adon's third meeting in the market square and Iki knew his brother was up to something. He needed to pay careful attention.

'Nothing today thanks my love. I am waiting for a friend.'

'Is she pretty?' The girl flirted, her eyes sparkling with mischief.

'Not as pretty as you my dear. What time do you finish?'

The girl lent forward and whispered in his ear. 'Around midnight and it is free for such a cutie as you, just don't tell the boss.' The girl indicated towards the barkeeper with a raised eyebrow. 'Meet you out the back.' She smiled seductively.

'Midnight it is then.' Iki whispered back with a charismatic smile. A sudden movement caught his eye as Adon stood to greet the Captain of the guard. The men shook with the warrior grip and Adon slapped the man on the back as they took a seat. Normally Iki would have thought nothing of the camaraderie; Adon was known for his touch with the common folk, but as the two men hunched over and spoke in soft tones, the Prince knew their plans were developing.

The sun reached its zenith as the pair sat talking, nervously looking over their shoulders from time to time. Iki waited until Adon finally finished his meeting and as his brother walked down the street, he stood to follow. He raised his hand in a casual salute to the barmaid and waited until Adon disappeared around the corner before following.

He had taken only a few steps into the cobblestoned laneway when Adon was upon him. 'Why are you following me brother?' The big man collected him by his collar and lifted him into the air before moving into the alley behind the tavern.

'Because Uriah told me to and for good measure it seems. Now put me down.'

'You are not going to ruin my plans Iki.'

Iki looked into Adon's eyes and saw something he had never witnessed in his brother before. There was a certain level of madness to his gaze and it unnerved him 'Brother, come now. You know I have to tell Uriah you are planning something.' Iki smiled and held his hands out innocently, palms up.

'No, you do not and you will not.' Adon thumped Iki against the stone wall, knocking the air from his lungs.

'Do not do anything rash Adon.' Iki nervously drew in a quick breath, his back ached now but he knew it was the least of his worries. Adon was a full head taller than Iki and held the younger prince aloft like a child, legs still dangling in the air.

Adon fought the urge to do any real harm to his brother. Deep in his consciousness his inner voice was screaming at him to put his Iki down, but there was another voice, a voice that growled in frustration, *he cannot let Uriah know, he must not let Uriah know.*

Adon looked around, covering Iki's mouth so he could not call out as he dragged his younger brother into the barn behind the tavern. He looked around frantically trying to find something to securely tie his brother with. He reasoned that once his mission was successful, he would come back and release Iki and triumphantly present the head of his enemy to Uriah.

Time seemed to stand still as he absentmindedly gagged Iki and tied him with leather reins from the stable. He was oblivious to the wild-eyed look his brother possessed and did not even take a second glance as he quietly closed the door to the barn leaving Iki behind in near darkness.

****

Salmah kissed Rahab one more time before tugging on the rope to check it was solid.

'Will you be back?' Rahab asked, keeping her tone as neutral as possible.

'I hope so, but I do not hold out much hope of hearing from Uriah and I need to report to Joshua.'

'Uriah will listen to reason. I am sure of it. He just needs to convince the King's council and his brothers that taking men from the walls with save their lives. I am sure Adon will not be easily swayed. He is a warrior through and through.'

'I will be back when the wall falls if not before. Stay here, collect up your family on the sixth night and whatever you do, do not leave the Inn. Joshua has said this is the only part of the wall that will not fall and I believe him. Please, trust me on this.' Salmah looked earnestly at Rahab, his concern obvious.

Rahab nodded and blew Salmah a kiss as he shimmied down the rope and disappeared from her sight. She closed her eyes and gave a silent prayer to the Goddess Asherah. There was an unsettled feeling the Innkeeper was struggling to overcome. She tied her apron and left the washroom for the main dining area knowing that her work would push her worries away at least for the time being.

Salmah hugged the shadows below the wall. He knew the guards were due to pass above Rahab's Inn at any moment so he watched and waited patiently for them.

Time seemed to stop entirely in the darkness. The lights of the city were far above and in the distance the fires burned amidst his own people. The young tribal leader felt a sense of loneliness as he waited, stranded amongst the in-between of Rahab's city and his own people who longed to establish themselves as free and prosperous folk once and for all.

He wondered again why the god of his people wished the death of the city of Jericho and prayed that there was another way for God to show his power and free His people.

Chapter 20

Iki could not decide if he was more afraid or outraged. Whatever Adon was up to, it was not going to be good and when Uriah found out about his unlawful incarceration, it was only going to get worse for his big brother.

Either way, Uriah had to know Adon was conspiring with the Captain of the guard about something and that he may well have lost his mind entirely in the process.

The youngest of three brothers had afforded the Prince plenty of experience in being the brunt of the jest. Uriah was smart, so very intelligent that Iki had never hoped to live up to such a high standard and Adon, well Adon was just huge, strong and a fierce fighting machine. That had left Iki with no other avenue of grandeur as a child except to be exceptionally resourceful and he excelled at that. If he could not be the strategist or the warrior, he had to be the spy or the thief or the lord of misdirection, whichever served its purpose best.

Right now, he needed to get free to report to Uriah. The brothers could sort out the power play or politics of it all later. Iki searched his surroundings. It was so very dark and he could barely see a few paces in front of him. He could smell the horses and hear them milling in their stalls. There was a small shaft of light that came through a high opening in the barn roof and Iki moved onto his knees so he could crawl over to the edge of the stalls. His only hope was to find a rake or wooden shovel close by or something sharp enough to cut through his bindings.

Adon had been careful, even methodical which was very out of character. Iki found his arms and legs not only tied, but tied together behind his back like a piece of mutton hanging from a spit roast.

The Prince could not straighten up. The tension on the rope that joined his feet to his hands was too tight. Instead he hopped, shimmied and wriggled his way on his knees with his back arched unnaturally so that the ropes did not cut too fiercely.

On a different day, under different circumstances it might have made for a comical sight, but today was not that day. The sweat dripped from his face and ran down his back, while his breathing continued to grow more difficult through the coarse fibres jammed down his throat.

Iki grunted as his knee struck a hard object but the depth of blackness made it impossible to see what he had discovered. The Prince rolled sideways with a heavy thud, onto the ground so that he could get his bound hands on the item and distinguish if it might be of any use.

It felt like eternity but after a concerted effort Iki found the item with his left hand. It was a wooden platter. His heart sank as he realised it would not be sharp enough to cut his leather bindings. Exhausted he collapsed onto the filthy dung smelling straw-covered floor and tried desperately to regain his breath and composure.

****

Nimal was not sure what had gotten into Adon but he was not complaining. Sitting around waiting for the Israelites to attack was demoralising and watching them prance around with their trumpets daily was just plain frustrating. How could Uriah sit by and not raise a hand? At least Adon was doing something.

It had taken a few days to collect the list of supplies the warrior had asked for. Nimal had ropes, grappling hooks, cooking oil in large clay jars and arrangements had been made with a collection of spies beyond the walls to supply the remainder of their requirements, all would ensure their plans could succeed.

Nimal was lost in thought as Adon approached. 'Are the men ready?'

'Yes Sir.'

'Now you are sure no one knows?' Adon frowned at the Captain of the Guard who moved from foot to foot uncomfortably under the big man's questioning gaze.

'I assure you Sir, if anyone of my men has said or even thought a word of this outside our group, I will skin him myself.' Adon waited for the silence to grow, measuring the Captain's words and body language. Satisfied he nodded his approval.

'Very well. Say the word Nimal.'

The Captain nodded to a young pimple faced boy with hair hanging over his eyes, who took off with the agility and speed of a field rabbit along the top of the wall.

Adon smiled to himself. 'They will not know what hit them.'

'Indeed Sir.' Nimal held a torch, ready to toss down to his men when the time came. The fire cast an eerie light on the Prince and the Captain felt a shiver run down his spine. 'May the Goddess favour us.'

Adon looked at Nimal as though he had grown and extra head but said nothing. The very uttering of the Goddess made the Prince feel like emptying his stomach contents, but he could not help but wonder why.

He had visited the shrine as a child and listened to the tutors who explained the ancient gods and goddesses of his people. They patiently told them they had and would continue to serve a great purpose amongst the poor and uneducated, but refined gentlemen like themselves need not take the ideology too seriously.

Yet Uriah was spooked over the Israelite's god and there was something deep in his own soul calling for divine power from a god with more violent tendencies. The Goddess was all about fertility and love and all that soft, impotent rubbish.

Love never won a war, fertility just brought more mouths to feed and cost good warriors their wages in support payments to whores. No, if there was a god, he needed power from now. It was not some pretty maiden in white robes or a philosophical god of goodness. He needed a god with guts and the power to drive out the invaders from his inherited lands. If there was such a god he was willing to swear fealty.

Adon was dragged from his melancholy as his men reached the bottom of the wall. 'Toss down the torches.' He called and burning sticks flared into the night all along the wall. The warrior could barely contain his excitement. It had been too long since he had fought the good fight and felt the adrenalin of combat through his veins.

 Chapter 21

Iki lay on the stable floor for what felt like eternity. Why was he so worried about what Adon was up to in any case? Uriah would be King after their father passed and Iki had no place in the Royal household except to be the runt of the litter.

If Jericho fell, he could just disappear into the night and travel the world. The thought raised his spirits momentarily until he realised he could hardly run off to anywhere tied up in a barn, covered in horse pee and hay and he had to admit that if Uriah died because he sat idly waiting for a rescue, even he would struggle to live with the guilt.

Iki was considering his options when he remembered the barmaid and their intended frolic. A wicked smile found its way through his uncomfortable gag. The Prince hefted the wooden platter and considered its weight as the horses moved quietly in their stalls.

The young barmaid washed her hands and smoothed her hair before untying her apron to signal the end of another long and tiring shift. There was a little part of her that wanted to just go home to her lumpy mattress and sleep the exhaustion away, but the Prince was waiting.

True, she would make no coin this night but gaining the favour of one of the Royal household was worth a little overtime. The petite girl knew she was attractive. With a fine waist and ample bosom there were few men who could resist her charms, but alluring the Prince permanently would take all her skills. She pondered her plans, drawing on her extensive experience as she walked behind the tavern to the stables.

The alley was poorly lit and there was very little moonlight to help guide her way. The clouds had gathered late in the day and held in the warmth making the evening balmy. The barmaid peered into the darkness and idly pulled her sleeves down from her shoulders so her top would drop lower over her cleavage.

There was no sign of the Prince. Had he stood her up? She grumbled at herself for the stupidity. She never expected to wed the Prince but she did believe she had a chance of becoming his well-paid and kept mistress.

How naive could she have been? Humiliation began to replace her anger. She pulled her sleeves back up over her shoulders with agitated vigour and prepared to leave the dark alley in favour of her bed after all. She was only a few paces from the main thoroughfare when she heard a crash in the stables and a horse neigh and stomp the ground.

It was none of her concern she told herself and turned back to continue her journey but a quiet voice spoke in her mind. *Someone might be hurt and you could get a great reward.* It was quickly followed by another voice. *And you could end up losing a hand if someone assumes you are breaking in.* It was as though an internal argument was taking place and she felt she had no control over it.

Another crash and more stomping hooves, this time louder and more urgent. The girl pushed caution aside and ran to the stables. She opened the doors into darkness, following the sound bravely as the frightened horses protested loudly.

She was only a few steps in when she stumbled over something large and unexpected on the floor. She sprawled face first onto the filthy smelling straw and dirt as the sound of an almost animalistic grunt reached her ears.

The girl tried to stand, but hands grabbed at her body. Her mind was racing as the screams exploded from her mouth without control or warning. She clawed at her assailant uncontrollably.

A torchlight reached the entrance and the girl spun around to see what was attacking her. On the floor, tied up like a piece of game was the Prince. His face was smeared with dirt and manure but the image was unmistakable. For a moment, the stable fell silent to her ears until the shouts of the tavern owner and staff forced their way into her consciousness.

'What on earth. Girl, why are you in here and who is this? What have you done to him?' The short and rather plump tavern owner frowned in the firelight as the man on the floor tried to struggle to his feet.

'I, I, I just heard a noise and came in to see what was happening. I tripped….'

'Maybe we should untie the fellow and ask him.' A tall and lanky woman with greying hair pulled back in a bun and wearing a long tunic moved forward, helping the girl to her feet but continuing to stare down at the man still tied up on the floor.

Iki stared back in disbelief. How long were they going to take to release him? How dim-witted could these people be? He grunted in agreement with the tall lady and twisted his body around trying to hold out his hands without tripping himself back over on his face. He knew he looked ridiculous, but he was desperate to be free of his bindings.

'I dunno. He could be dangerous.' The tavern owner speculated. 'Maybe he has been tied up here by some stall holder who has gone to get the guard?'

'The guard have been nowhere in sight today, so that could be true.' The woman joined in considering their options.

The barmaid finally found her voice and her courage. 'Are you both daft? This is the Prince, I would know his face anywhere. Release him and find out what is going on.' She blushed at her admission of admiration and her blatant abuse of her employer's intelligence. Iki raised an eyebrow in response.

'Now girly, no need to be rude. You sure?' Her boss frowned, waving his torch in front of Iki's face to get a clear view.

'Yes Sir, absolutely positive. There might even be a reward in releasing him.' The girl ventured, returning a questioning eyebrow in Iki's direction.

The Prince nodded fervently in agreement, grunting and silently praying they would finally make a decision to let him go. The girl realised he was trying to speak and lent forward removing his gag at last.

'The barmaid is correct. I am Ikidran, third royal Prince. I need to get to the Palace, immediately.

It is urgent, untie me and whatever you do, do not call the City Guard.'

'But if you are the Prince and you not be up to mischief then why can't we call the guard?' The tavern owner spoke slowly, almost painstakingly as he rubbed his chin pondering his options.

Iki sighed. 'Because if you do, you will probably end up dead. They are up to something and I need to let the King and my brother know. Now untie me.' Iki held out his hands again. He kept the fact his father was still incapacitated to himself.

It took a moment to send someone for a knife from the kitchen to cut the bindings but Iki was finally on his way to find Uriah, the young barmaid in tow.

'What is your name?' They walked quickly and conversation was difficult but the Prince wanted to know the name of the woman who freed him and was apparently infatuated with him enough to know exactly who he was all along.

'Nalia.'

'Well thank you Nalia, remind me I owe you a royal feast when this is done.'

'What is *this* anyway?' Nalia frowned at the Prince's back as she virtually ran to keep up.

'Secret royal stuff, you know, the type of boring political games that go on in royal circles.' The girl shrugged trying to remain unconcerned but Iki could see she was intrigued. 'If everything goes well, I can bring you up to date after the fact, but for now, I need to get to my brother.'

There were absolutely no guards to be found as they quickly made their way to the Palace. Nalia struggled to keep up as Iki took the front steps three at a time. She watched him from behind and smiled as the muscles in his legs carried him to the top. 'I will come back for you shortly.' He called down. 'Find her somewhere to freshen up.' He said absently to the first royal servant who caught his eye as he rushed up the hall towards Uriah.

The servant frowned at the dirt covered barmaid and then cleared his features almost immediately, as though the request was not so unusual after all. Nalia wondered how many stray and dirty barmaids the Prince had brought home to be 'freshened up', then decided with Iki's looks there had probably been too many to count

****

'What do you mean you lost him?' Uriah was standing, hands crossed firmly against his chest. Anyone would think he ruled the place Iki thought, then laughed to himself. He was commander now, even if it felt foreign to kneel to him, Uriah was the man for the job.

'I did not exactly lose him. He grabbed me, tied me up and for a minute I thought he might seriously hurt me. He is teetering on the edge of a berserk rage brother.'

'What is his plan then?'

'No real idea except he has the whole Guard on side and they are nowhere to be seen on the streets tonight. Whatever is planned, it is going on right now.'

Uriah ran from the room, Iki close behind. 'Royal guard to me, now! Find me the Commander.' A tall guard with a short beard saluted and jogged down the corridor toward the barracks. 'Run like your arse is on fire man!' Uriah called after him and the soldier's pace increased significantly.

 Chapter 22

Salmah waited for the guards to pass but no one came. He rubbed his chin as he considered the reasons and prayed Rahab was alright. There was little he could do now. He needed to see Joshua. Uriah should have reported back his plans by now, yet no word had come from the Palace. Joshua would have no mercy on any-one who manned the wall when the time came and time was running out.

It was late when Salmah arrived in camp to see Deshaun tossing another log into the fire. The Levite smiled when he saw his friend and jogged over to greet him. 'Good to see the spy lives.'

'A spy is only a spy when the enemy does not know who they are Deshaun. Uriah knows me on sight now.'

'True. Are you here long?'

'No idea my friend. That will be up to Joshua. Is he awake?'

'When is he not?' Salmah nodded as he made his way to Joshua's tent. The old man was too old now. He needed his rest but the pressure of leadership was great and the burning desire to see Israel established in the Canaanite lands before he died was what kept the old man from dying, Salmah was sure of it.

Salmah stopped as he walked to meet Joshua. He took in the tents, the cook-fires and the livestock that milled around and smiled to himself. Soon the people of Israel would have homes made of stone and lands to farm. He wanted this for his people as much as anyone but at what price?

He composed himself and continued forward into Joshua's tent. The old man did not look up as he spoke. 'I wondered when you might return Salmah.'

'Did you doubt me?' Salmah waited for a response. He knew Joshua did not like him spending time with Rahab and he questioned his future amongst the Israelites if they refused her. *Judah may yet have to make a nation unto itself*, he kept his thoughts to himself.

'It is not me you need to please Salmah, it is your God.'

'You and I will have to agree to disagree on how we see my God Joshua, but that is a discussion for another day. Uriah has not returned an answer, yet I am sure he will call his men from the wall and surrender to our forces. Do I still have your assurance no one dies if this happens?'

'I question your loyalties Salmah. You seem to care too much for these people.'

'I care too much for all people Joshua. If our God is the father of all creation, of all the people then surely, he also cares about the people of Jericho?

'Possibly, or maybe he wants us to show them the way to our God and some may perish in the process.'

Salmah shook his head gently. 'Do you seek death that desperately Joshua?'

The old man seemed shocked. 'You have grown bold Salmah. Your time with the whore is corrupting your soul. I pray God will shed his light upon you.'

'You have not answered my question Joshua. Will the people of Jericho be spared if Uriah removes his men from the battlements and surrenders the city when the wall falls? Or has it all been a ploy, merely a distraction to keep Uriah's attention?'

Joshua sat in silence a moment, somehow lost in thought. Salmah began to believe he had nodded off making his words seem even stronger and more powerful when he spoke. 'The Lord has offered mercy but the Prophets say war and death are inevitable. Not all men seek the peaceful path Salmah.'

Salmah turned to leave but paused looking back at Joshua. 'Uriah will.'

As he left the tent he felt unsettled, as though the old man was keeping something from him. If God could tear down the walls, why did he wait? Salmah allowed his anger to wash over him and as the frustration passed, the words came into his mind. *Time affords choice.* Salmah had no idea where the thought had sprung from but it made sense.

If God stormed in and brought the walls down, thousand would die. If he made a fanfare and paraded around the walls for days, then he gave the people of Jericho a choice. This was His plan. The walls would fall, but the people still had a choice to live or to die.

Salmah made his way to his tent but not before stopping off to see Deshaun once more. His mind was racing, something was not quite right. Joshua knew more than he was sharing and the lack of guards on the walls in Jericho left the young soldier feeling uneasy.

Deshaun saw Salmah approaching and greeted his friend with a bowl of steaming stew and flat bread. 'Here, have something to eat. You look like you need it.'

Salmah took the offering and smiled. 'You have no idea. It feels like I have not eaten in a week. I am tired Deshaun. All the spying, all the secrets, all the scheming. Why God does not just wave his hand and open the gates, or speak into the minds of the people of Jericho, I do not know. Why all the cloak and dagger secrecy? I am at a loss my friend. Games, too many games.'

Deshaun patted his friend on the back. 'What exactly do you mean?' The younger Levite was genuinely confused.

'Joshua is keeping something from us Deshaun, I am sure of it and when I left the city, there were no guards on the walls. I think Joshua knows something and he is not sharing it with me.'

'You should get some rest.' Deshaun pointed to their tent. 'Maybe you have been playing too hard and worn yourself out man.' Deshaun smiled knowingly.

'You might be right. I think rest is a good idea. Stay alert though my friend. Something is not right, mark my words.'

Deshaun nodded as Salmah pushed himself to his feet and made his way to his tent, scooping a spoonful of stew into his mouth as he went. It was late and the encampment was quiet as Salmah finished his food, slipped off his sandals and allowed himself the solitude of his narrow, hard bed once more.

****

Joshua watched the boy leave. He was growing head-strong and the old man could not help but wonder if that trait would be his saving grace or his undoing. He should have told Salmah what he knew, what was to come to pass but he could not bring himself to. It would change nothing.

There were those who would expect him to warn everyone. To sit by and do nothing was to bring about the pain himself, but Joshua had lived a long time now and he knew that when prophecy was shared it was a forgone conclusion and no matter what he did, it would come to pass.

There were Priests amongst the Israelites who did not agree with him, but they knew better than to go against his leadership. Men and women would die on both sides but in the end the Lord would be victorious and that was the entire point.

God had punished his own people for their lack of faith and this fact had troubled the young Joshua but so much time had passed since he had first laid eyes on the Promised Land.

At first Joshua had asked the Prophet why God had denied the other tribal leaders access to the land of the Canaanites. Why had they all been forced to roam the desert for a generation? The answer had come to him in time for it was time that meant nothing to God.

He was all around in the clouds, upon the soil, in the spirit of His people and he was eternal. All men die, it is the legacy they leave behind that really mattered.

Joshua pushed himself to his feet, lifting the candle from his low table as he made his way to his hard and unforgiving bed. Getting up and down from the ground was growing tiresome but the old man knew it would not be for much longer. His time was short.

He blew out the candle and waited for sleep to overtake his tired and aching body but the images would not give him peace. 'Your will be done Lord,' he whispered as he pushed the images aside and drifted into a dreamless sleep.

Chapter 23

'What are you doing Moloch?' Asherah stood with her arms crossed watching her brother intently.

'I have no idea what you speak of Sister.' Moloch smiled, noting the growing frustration on Asherah's face. He knew how much she hated him referring to her as his own bloodline.

'You know exactly what I mean Moloch. Stop it. You are meddling with Yahweh's plans.' The Goddess's arms had moved to her hips now and if there was any power in a scowl, Moloch would have been shaking in his boots. Instead his laughter rang out.

'You are so naïve at times. I am not meddling with the Father's plans, I am playing my part in them.' Asherah almost gasped her surprise but managed to muster some composure before allowing herself to feed her brother with more ammunition to taunt her with.

'No, not possible. Father would never allow you to bring death like this.'

'As I said naïve. You are still young Asherah and you have spent too much time whoring and making babies and growing trees to see the whole picture.'

'And I suppose you have the complete story all mapped out.' Asherah knew Moloch was goading her, but she was on a roll now and could not stop herself. 'Yahweh is full of love, not fire and brimstone as demons like you would have the people believe.'

'Demons, well I like that.' The laughter did not reach Moloch's eyes. 'The sons of the Father are demons while the daughters are Goddesses. How convenient. We get to do His dirty work, while you pretty little butterflies get to heal and love and grow. I am not a mistake Asherah. I, just like all Father's creations have a purpose to fulfil.'

Asherah was speechless. She had sensed Moloch wielding his hate upon the people of Jericho for days and no matter how hard she had tried, she had not been able to intervene in time to stop his plans from taking form.

There was a reason she did not live amongst her brethren. There had been a time when Heaven had been the most peaceful and beautiful place to reside but that time had long since passed, so long ago that Asherah could barely recall the happiness she had experienced there.

Now she stayed away, preferring to live amongst her worshippers in Jericho but now her haven was being destroyed. She had blamed Moloch, but deep down she knew her Father had birthed this plan long ago, yet hearing that Moloch believed he did Father's work, well that was a hard cherry to swallow.

Why would Yahweh do that? Asherah ignored her brother's gloating as she took in her surroundings. She had tracked Moloch into the house of the gods. Yes, he was right to some degree. Yahweh was the creator of all things but the gods and goddesses of Heaven were strong and there was always one faction fighting against another for power over the people of this world.

Moloch was called a demon amongst the host of heaven, but in truth he was no less divine than she was. The blood of gods ran through his veins as much as it did through hers; it was just easier to disown him if she thought of him as a demon, somehow different from her.

They were not floating amongst the clouds as the people of the world below thought gods did. The House of the Gods was more than a place amongst the stars. Heaven was here and now but nowhere all at the same time. It was neither cold nor warm. It was neither heavy nor light, it just was.

No one had ever really needed to explain the phenomenon to Asherah, she had just always understood that the gods were like air, they could travel wherever and whenever they wanted and take form as anything they chose.

Asherah opened her hand and produced a flower, dropping it into nothingness as she pondered the Father's plans. The gods had been unsettled for so long it was impossible to date. Yahweh's plan was to unite the people under One God, Him.

Asherah was happy to follow the plan but others were not. She had always believed Moloch was amongst the opposition, but now here he was telling her he was part of the process. The thought that Yahweh had employed Moloch's tactics was unsettling to say the least. Asherah composed herself.

'I think you might have misunderstood your role Moloch. If Father has called you to aid in His plans then you have gone outside of His guidelines.'

'Why!' Moloch interrupted. 'Because I have sent opposition against the Israelites? Because I have encouraged the Canaanites to stand up for themselves? If Hamilkot were not under your power, then they would already be at war. Are you so stupid as to believe Father does not use violence to bring about His plans?'

'Not stupid, or naïve Moloch. I simply have hope and faith that there is another way.'

'Then it is you who go against the Father Asherah, not I.' Moloch looked earnestly at his sister and Asherah felt uncomfortable under his gaze.

'I pray you are wrong.' As Asherah spoke the words she could not help but wonder who she was to send such a prayer to.

****

Adon looked from left to right and nodded to his men. It was time. Time to bring the fight to the invading force. No more prancing around the walls blowing horns and making threats that ate away the spirit of his people. Uriah might be the diplomat, but he was the warrior and the time for talking was over.

Nimal smirked at his Prince, an eerie image even for Adon. He knew the man had a grudge against Uriah. Something about the whore Rahab. The man's motives were not pure, this he knew but he needed men who were willing to die for the cause and Nimal had provided such men.

It was hours after midnight and Adon knew the sentries would be growing tired. He had spent days hatching this plan and surprise was everything. His thoughts drifted to Iki and the Prince could not help but wonder what had come over him.

There had been a moment when he had been willing to slit the throat of his little brother. How could he have contemplated such a deed? Everyone loved Iki, the clown Prince who had managed to avoid both the diplomatic training of Uriah and the fighting Adon had experienced. He had grown up in better times, when the Canaanites had no need to wage war. How could Iki understand what he was about to do? Still the discomfort in knowing he nearly killed his favourite brother and closest friend was difficult to shake.

'They won't know what hit 'em Sir.' Nimal spoke quietly as they approached the tents.

The layout of the dwellings was ingenious Adon noted. His people had never known this type of strategy; too many years fighting from the city walls or cutting and running on open ground not far from the safety of the tall stone ramparts.

Adon considered the camp. It had been difficult to judge the right place to attack from the walls of

Jericho and now Adon took his time before giving direction to his men. There were wagons lined up making a wall to prevent livestock from roaming. The people slept below the wagons and the Prince knew these were peasants, not soldiers. He had no desire to hurt any innocent women or children, it was the leaders and fighting men he sought.

Beyond the lines of wagons and livestock, the tents of the soldiers could be seen. The defence of placing the fighting men behind the people was not lost on Adon. He could not make up his mind if it was genius or cowardice. Something in his heart told him it was the latter, but in his own mind he knew it was incredibly clever.

The soldier's tents were arranged in circles around camp fires. Each circle of tents formed part of a larger circle that surrounded the accommodation of the leaders, the Priests and no doubt that big golden box the Israelites marched around the city walls every day. Adon promised himself that the box was going to end up in flames if it was the last act he could manage.

The warrior pointed to the soldier's tents and Nimal nodded, making hand signals for his men. As they walked amongst the wagons Adon scanned the sleeping forms to ensure there were no surprises waiting for him. He knew it would not take long for someone to sound the alarm. Every tenth man carried a lit torch ready to set fire to the camp. It was only a matter of moments before someone saw them approaching.

Adon did not have to wait long. They were almost upon the first camp fire when a young man who had been on sentry duty turned around to see the torch light flickering in the night. 'Who goes there?'

'Your worst nightmare son.' Adon replied as he charged forward, releasing his throwing knife, taking the boy in the throat. He was barely old enough to grow a beard Adon noticed as he retrieved his blade.

# Chapter 24

Uriah made it to the wall just in time to see a line of fired torches fanning out around the Israelite's encampment. 'What in the Goddess's name does he think he is doing?'

'Thinking is not something Adon is renowned for.' Iki shrugged at Uriah's glare. He knew his humour was out of place at such a time, yet what else could he do. People were going to die this night and he had been tied up and incapacitated by his own brother. He felt somehow hopeless and impotent from the experience.

'What are your orders Sir?' The Commander of the Royal Guard waited nearby. Uriah could see he was itching to get his men into the fray.

'I am afraid my brother has taken on an unwinnable quest Commander. I know you want to join him, but I cannot possibly lose the City Guard and the Royal Guard in one night of stupidity.'

His Commander looked disappointed but nodded his agreement.

'He is going to get himself killed.' Iki whispered.

'It is not your fault Iki.' Uriah tried to comfort his youngest brother. 'It is just his way. Adon has never been happy to stand by and wait on a peaceful outcome.'

'That does not make it easier Uriah. If he had not seen me following him. If he had not overpowered me…' Iki let his words drift off as melancholy took over.

'He still has a chance brother. He is a skilled warrior, if anyone can manage to survive such a pitched battle, it is Adon.' Uriah looked out at the fired encampment as he spoke and allowed his own guilt to wash over him. 'I can understand his frustration.' The Prince spoke softly. 'If this is anyone's fault it is mine. I should have sent word to Joshua that I agreed to his terms earlier. Now there will be no surrender.' Uriah sighed.

'What do mean?' Iki frowned. 'This is all on Adon, not you.'

'It will make no difference to the Israelites. If the roles were reversed we would assume the worst. They will expect to meet a hostile force when they breach the walls.' Uriah watched the carnage unfold. The fires broke out amongst the tents and the screams of the dying rode upon the night air.

Uriah turned to the Commander. 'Ready whatever men we have left. Gather as many able-bodied civilians as you can find. We have less than three days left to prepare.'

****

You must stop him Rahab. Seek out Uriah and stop him. There is another way. I will provide it. Bring the Prince to me at the shrine. Rahab stifled a scream as she awoke from her dream. There was sweat running down her back and her heart was racing like she had run a marathon. The images left in her mind were painful and for a moment she believed them to be only a nightmare until the sound of screaming and the smell of smoke came to her.

The Priestess almost stumbled as she raced down the ladder from her loft bed and made her way to the window in the darkness. There was an eerie red glow filtering through as she approached and the line of red light made a pathway for her to follow.

As she reached the window her heart leapt into her throat. The Israelite encampment was aflame with the glow of bright orange fire. It was difficult to make out what was going on but the blaze was so high and so fierce that anyone within a hundred paces would have been roasted alive.

Rahab could not think clearly. All she kept hearing were the words of the Goddess in her mind and the screams of the dying drifting to her senses. She shook herself from her confusion and dressed as quickly as she could.

Thoughts of Salmah were with her now and she begged the Goddess to save him from the fires. Her heart ached to see him and know he was safe, but she knew Uriah was who she needed to find right now. She questioned if he would see her at this late hour and wondered why he had risked the lives of all of Jericho with such a reckless attack on the Israelites.

It took only moments for Rahab to dress and leave the confines of her Inn. As she walked the streets toward the Palace she was almost overcome with the smoke that drifted on the light night breeze toward the city. People were standing on the walls, watching the carnage unsure if they should celebrate a victory or prepare for defeat.

The Priestess knew getting past the guards on such a night was going to be difficult but she had to believe the Goddess would find a way. She thought about what she would say to Uriah. All she knew was that Asherah wanted her to bring him to the Shrine; but how?

****

Nimal watched Adon charge the boy by the fire. It was over in a heartbeat, the young soldier never stood a chance against the huge warrior Prince. The Captain of the Guard smiled as the blood drained from the wound and life left the boy's eyes.

There would be many more this night and Nimal looked forward to seeing each-and-every death. The Israeli scum would finally die and Jericho would be free to open the gates to trade once more.

Nimal was no coward but he kept pace safely behind the Prince. It was obvious to anyone who had eyes that the big man was a force to be reckoned with and the less likely place to take a sword to the gut would be riding Adon's wake of destruction.

The camp exploded into confusion as the cook fires were scattered and the torches set the oiled animal skin tents aflame. Adon's orders had been clear to all the men of the city guard. The civilians that skirted the camp and their livestock were to be spared. Nimal liked the idea. Plenty of women to fire the men's loins and enough food to feed the city for years would be the spoils.

The Captain ducked under a wild sword swing and gutted the soldier easily. The Israelites were fit and lean but they were unskilled with weapons and the bodies of the dead were piling up around the clearing. Nimal watched the Prince making ground toward the large tent that marked the centre of the camp. The warrior was not the smartest Nimal had ever seen but it did not take a genius to work out that tent belong to someone or something important.

Time seemed to stand still for the Captain as they slowly made ground. The fire was growing intense and Nimal could feel the hairs on his legs and arms beginning to shrivel with the heat. 'We have to leave Sir. The fire is too hot. It will kill us all.' Nimal yelled above the screams of the dying but the Prince did not respond.

With less than ten paces remaining to the main tent Nimal began to reconsider his options. He scanned the undergrowth for a break in the wall of fire that now surrounded them. His loyalties were being tested. Run for safety or remain with the warrior who inspired the revolt.

Nimal's eyes darted from side to side as fear crept into his spirit. The Captain nearly leapt out of his own skin when the tent flat sprung open and men began to swarm out like ants. They wore no armour and carried only spears and short swords. The force split into two lines, running left and right and circling around the small group of men who had followed Adon.

Nimal needed no encouragement. His instincts took over and before the circle could be completed, the Captain of the city guard disappeared in the haze of smoke and ran for the only piece of shrubbery that was not fully aflame. He jumped over the low bushes and never looked back, not for a moment. In his mind he knew that Adon was likely already dead; there were just too many of them.

# Chapter 25

The smoke cleared as the sun rose over the walls of Jericho. It would have been a beautiful and somewhat peaceful scene if not for the bodies that littered the encampment. Salmah walked the entire perimeter with a sense of desolation he could not shake.

None of this should have happened. It was his fault, he knew. If he had not been so distracted with Rahab he would have been constantly chasing Uriah for a decision and communicating with Joshua.

Why Uriah would authorise an attack puzzled him. From everything that Rahab had shared about the Prince and with having met him, it just did not seem to suit his personality. Salmah wiped the blood from his cheek as he recalled the night before. He had known something was amiss when he had visited Joshua and as he had headed to his bed he had not been able to sleep.

He had been tossing and turning when an image had come to him. Nothing like this had ever happened to the young man before. Who gets visions when they are wide awake? It was as though he were watching a dream but fully aware he was experiencing one. There was fire and Joshua was dead, his eyes gouged out of his head by the Captain of the guard who had wanted to kill Rahab the night Uriah had come for her.

At first Salmah had dismissed the images as a ridiculous hallucination or worse still, his own aggression toward the old man manifesting but no matter how hard he had tried to push the memory aside and get some sleep, it simply would not leave him. Eventually Salmah had awoken Joshua with his vision and the old man had called the Prophets to him.

Apparently, there had been no vision from God, not to the Prophets, not to Joshua himself but Salmah had felt uneasy about the old man's manner. He was keeping something from him, he knew but to his credit, instead of dismissing the visions as dreams or make-believe, the leader of the Israeli nation had gathered additional men to his tent and set extra men on watch. There was not a camp fire without a sentry when the attack had come. Still, so many had died.

Salmah rubbed more blood away from the still weeping wound on his face. The big man had been good, better than any warrior Salmah had ever fought. His people were not known for their sword craft and Salmah was no exception but he had been fortunate in his youth. His father had been a slave in Egypt before the exodus and had been hand-picked to train with the noble combatants who competed in stick fighting as a sport.

The prizes were opulent and the notoriety even more appealing for the younger nobles and Salmah's father had taken a beating until he had gained the skill to train the young nobles without sustaining broken bones.

Salmah smiled as he recalled his father's training sessions. As a young boy, he had asked why he needed to learn to fight when they were alone and wandering the desert. His father had merely said 'why not?'

Why not indeed. Salmah smiled again. His father had saved his life more than once now and he had the Egyptians to thank for passing on the skill. When the big man had levelled his sword, Salmah had known instantly how well trained he was. He balanced perfectly on the balls of his feet, his sword did not waver and he had watched Salmah like a hawk, aware of his surroundings, yet focussed and undistracted.

Salmah had tossed his short sword aside and the warrior had smirked at him. The expression did not reach his eyes and the memory sent a shiver down his spine once more. There had been a madness in those eyes that belied the focus the warrior showed, but Salmah had pushed the thought aside and hefted his spear.

Each thrust of the warrior's blade was pushed aside by the spinning and thrusting spear. The big man had begun to tire while Salmah was lean and fast. In time an opening in the warrior's defences had become evident. He favoured his right sword hand and protected his left side well, yet when pushed back hard and fast, he would leave his right hip exposed.

Salmah had waited patiently, watching the move over and over to be sure it was not a one off and he was not feigning. Satisfied the lack of defence was legitimate, Salmah had pushed the big man back with a series of jabs and arcs with the shaft of his spear. Finally, he had taken the blow with the spearhead that took the warrior just above his groin.

The blood was bright red and fast running but the big man had growled like a cornered cat and lunged forward. Salmah had not expected the move. In hindsight, he knew he should have; the man was built like a bullock and the madness in his eyes had never left him. The blade had nicked his cheek and the angry welt was still oozing blood. Salmah had stepped back as the warrior slumped to the ground, chest heaving.

'Luckily they do not all fight like you lad.' Of all the words to utter with your dying breath, Salmah had found this strange, almost unnerving. It was as though the words could not have been his own.

All the other soldiers were dead and everyone had stopped to watch Salmah fight the only remaining warrior. Salmah had knelt next to the man and waited with him until he died.

 Chapter 26

Rahab had waited for the rest of the night and into the early hours of the morning. She wanted to return to her Inn, to make sure Salmah was safe, to open for the morning and to pretend that none of this had ever happened, but she knew she could not.

The Priestess leant against the wall on the top step of the Palace entrance, drifting in and out of a light sleep. Servants ran around preparing for something special but no one would tell Rahab what was going on and the Royal guard had vanished. Surely Uriah had not taken his own guard into the encampment to attack the Israelites?

Without the guards to stop her, she was tempted to sneak in but after last night's craziness, she was concerned someone might be likely to kill first and ask questions later.

'Rahab, is that you?'

Rahab looked up to see Danal standing over her, hands on her hips. 'Danal. Thank the Goddess. I have to see Uriah.'

'Hi Danal, so nice to see you. How have you been?' Danal answered, replanting her hands on her hips in frustration.

'I am sorry Danal. Did I hurt your feelings? Your feelings are so important of course when we are at war with the Israelites and men are dead all over the ground, the stink still wafting over us like a sand storm.' Rahab had been told as a child she did not suffer fools gladly and today it seemed nothing had changed. 'I will offer you meaningless pleasantries after I get this mess sorted out, if that is alright with you?'

Danal just stared at her friend, mouth open for what felt to Rahab like an eternity before she finally shook herself back to the present. 'I get your point, but I have not seen you for days and you should still learn some manners you know.' She did not wait for an answer. 'Uriah is not back yet.'

'So, the idiot did raid the encampment?' Rahab blurted out loudly before she realised this was not the time or place for such a discussion. She looked over her shoulder to see if any of the servants had heard her. Thankfully they appeared to be busy rushing about their business.

'No, he did not. His idiot brother did.' Whispered Danal before seeing Rahab's confusion and clarifying. 'Adon.'

'Did Uriah join him?' Rahab suddenly felt afraid for her childhood friend.

'I do not believe so, but I have not been officially informed. All I know is he is on his way back here soon, hence the rush of activity. Come with me. I cannot guarantee he will see you, but you cannot stand out here any longer.'

'Thank you Danal.' Danal frowned at Rahab, trying to decide if she was being sarcastic again. 'No, really, thanks. My backside was beginning to go numb on this hard stone step.' Rahab smiled and Danal returned the gesture.

The young women walked through the entrance, down a hall and past the extravagant ball room that was used by Hamilkot for all the fancy functions he held; or did hold before he drifted into his mysterious sleep. Rahab suddenly wondered how the old King was doing.

'Where is Hamilkot's room?'

'You cannot visit the King Rahab, there is no way his physician is going to let anyone in to see him.'

'I might not be a noble Danal, but the staff here all know me well. How about you let me give it a try? I am forced to wait for an *audience* with his *lordship* in any case, so why not? I am a Priestess after all.' Rahab smiled mischievously and Danal was reminded of some of their escapades as children, when Rahab had permission to play in the Palace grounds with the noble families. They had been fabulous times, with no distinction between classes. She wondered when that had changed and honestly could not recall with any certainty.

'I will show you where but I will have nothing to do with your visit. Uriah will kill me.'

'He would do no such thing and you know it. How are the two of you going anyway? When is he going to marry you?' Rahab watched her friend's face and saw the discomfort. 'Is everything alright Danal? You have not gotten yourself with child or something silly like that?

'Not likely with Uriah.' Danal tried to keep the scorn from her voice.

'What are you talking about?' It had always been assumed that Uriah would marry Danal. Well she had always assumed it anyway. When it became obvious Uriah had to marry to sire an heir and that nobility would be enforced, she had bowed out in favour of her most nobly born friend.

'I really would rather not talk about it now Rahab.'

'Maybe not now, but we must talk as soon as I get back from seeing Hamilkot. It looks like it is time you told Uriah who is in charge. We will talk soon. Agreed?' Rahab waited for Danal to make eye contact once more. She could see the girl was close to tears. 'What is it Danal, tell me now.' She shook her head.

'I will see you after, I promise.' They had kept talking while they walked and Rahab realised she was close to Hamilkot's apartment. Danal pointed to the dark timber doors at the end of the left hand corridor. 'He is in there. I will send someone to get you as soon as Uriah agrees to see you.' Danal turned and rushed off. Rahab could see she was holding back a river of tears. Confused, the Priestess forced herself to focus on what needed her attention now. She could not explain why, but she knew that she needed to check in on the King but she had no idea why.

Chapter 27

Asherah relaxed as she saw Rahab open the door to Hamilkot's apartment. Moloch might have claimed to be doing Yahweh's work, but he could not be trusted and the Goddess knew he had tried to harm Hamilkot, she simply was not sure how.

There were portions of Moloch's argument that the Goddess agreed with. For instance, there was no doubt that Heaven was awash with factions.

The legends claimed that Yahweh was the creator of all the universe and that the lessor gods, or angels as the humans often called them had been his children; like all sons and some daughters, they did not all see eye to eye with their father and so it was in Heaven.

The Goddess consoled herself with the knowledge that Yahweh was all-knowing and that He had realised his progeny would stray from His path over time. She had to believe that he had developed the grand plan to reunite Heaven and earth under one god, Himself.

Yet this prophecy was not believed or vindicated by all. There were those amongst the host that considered themselves more powerful and fought for dominance. There were others who were jealous of the care and attention Yahweh bestowed upon the humans and plotted to see their demise. She believed Moloch slotted into this faction and often wondered why Yahweh had not put an end to his meddling on earth eons ago.

Asherah pondered the prophecy that had been shared with her so many years before. It mattered not to her how the other gods cared to consider it, she believed the grand plan to be the only option for the survival of humanity and for peace in Heaven therefore she would do all she could to ensure the correct outcome was achieved.

For the Prophecy to be fulfilled, Rahab and Salmah must unite and Uriah along with his father must be saved from the destruction of Jericho. These two ancestral lines would come together in the future as the Hittite and Israeli nations and were destined to ensure the birth of the bringer of peace. So much relied on this pivotal moment in time that she could not help but wonder if Moloch sought to change the future with his constant scheming.

Asherah pushed the troubling thought from her mind. Yahweh had a plan and she simply needed to play her part. Right now, she needed to guide Salmah back before it was too late.

****

Nimal's mind was racing. Dawn was approaching and he knew he only had moments left before the ropes would be pulled from the wall and his only escape back to the city would be closed to him. Yet what was he going to say to Uriah when he returned? How was he to avoid the death penalty?

No matter what, for now he had to make sure he made it back into Jericho before it was too late and he was trapped outside the walls, easy pickings for the Israelites. Nimal hugged the shadows as he made it to the wall of the city. The darkness was giving way to the rising sun as the Captain reached the knotted rope.

As Nimal began the long climb to the ramparts he decided that Adon had not really thought this part of the plan through. Or had the big man never intended on returning? Nimal suddenly wondered. Surely not. Suicide was not in the Prince's bloodline he assured himself until he reached the half way point. He stopped, hanging from a knotted handhold, trying to regain his breath. The muscles in his arms ached and began to shake with the fatigue.

No, Adon would not have considered anyone incapable of climbing the knotted rope to safety. He was strong and still young but Nimal was flabby and older and he had to admit, terribly unfit.

The sun crested the battlements as Nimal dragged himself onto the top, shimmying into the darkened shade of the closest wall. It was only a matter of time before the Royal guard found him, so rest was not an option. The Captain wiped the sweat from his brow and pushed on, crawling on his hands and knees into the darkness of a weapons storeroom.

He needed time to compose his story before reporting to Uriah. The younger Prince Ikitan knew

Nimal had been helping Adon and the only way to turn this misfortune around was to make Adon the hero and Uriah the coward, but how?

Chapter 28

Rahab watched the physician suspiciously. The man was sweating unnaturally and the Priestess wondered over it. She smiled at him, offering him some comfort but it seemed only to add to his agitation.

'You seem somewhat nervous Malic. Are you feeling well?'

'Yes of course my dear.' The Physician tried to think quickly. Why was the Priestess here? Did she harbour suspicions? The accident with the medicine had not been the only slip up on his part during the care of the King and try as he might, Malic could not fathom where his mind had been.

He had tested himself for the aging sickness and this was not the cause. Adding an assistant to his preparation had helped, yet still there had been more incidents the physician cared not to think about.

'Have you discovered the cause of the King's affliction?' Rahab was trying hard not to push, but the beads of sweat kept appearing on Malic's face.

'No, alas I have no idea. Hamilkot is not improving, but neither is he getting worse.' It was not a lie. There had been several occasions when the King had grown unstable, but Malic had recognised the symptoms instantly and attended to the remedies immediately.

On each occasion, he knew the King had been poisoned and in all cases, he had been the attending physician. It was as though large blanks had formed in his own memory for each occasion. He dared not tell a soul, least of all Uriah.

Yet now here was Rahab. Malic had known her as a child and knew her now by reputation. Uriah trusted her and if she was sent by the Prince, Malic felt his excuses would not be enough to save him.

'Do you mind if I take a look?' Rahab stood to conduct an examination.

'Child, what can a Priestess do that a Physician has not already done.' As soon as the worlds left his lips Malic knew he had made a mistake.

Rahab drew herself up and took a deep breath. She knew she should let the matter slide by her yet it had never been in her nature to do such a passive thing. 'Well I am not sure Malic,' Rahab tried unsuccessfully to keep the sarcasm from her words, 'but us mere Priestesses do train in earth remedies. The Goddess is quite thorough with our education. Contrary to popular demand, we heal more than a man's waning libido.'

'I am sure that will not be necessary Priestess. The Prince has entrusted me with the King's care; unless you are here on his orders?' Malic felt suddenly bold. The sweating had disappeared and he felt a surge of warmth in his chest that pushed him on.

Rahab ignored the man and felt for the King's pulse. It was steady but the Priestess felt her unease rising. 'Really Priestess. I must insist. Do I need to get a guard to remove you?' Malic threatened.

Rahab took a risk and quickly lent in to smell the King's breath and push one eyelid back to see the colour of his eyes. 'I believe the Royal guard are otherwise occupied so good luck with getting assistance.' Rahab smiled as Malic began to fidget. She was right, something was amiss. Malic rushed to the door of the King's apartments and began calling for anyone who would listen.

'That will not be necessary *Physician.'* Rahab did not hide her disdain. 'I am leaving. I have a prior engagement with Uriah. I am sure the Prince will be overjoyed when I express my opinion over his father's care.' Rahab smiled as the man's eyes nearly exploded from their sockets. He was hiding something, of that she was sure.

In truth, she had no idea if Uriah would even grant her an audience after the massacre from the previous night, but she had to tell him what she had found in Hamilkot's rooms and more importantly, what the Goddess wanted her to do.

Rahab pushed past the Physician and through the open doorway where he had moments ago been demanding help from guards who were nowhere to be seen. She left the King's apartment with no real destination in mind. Danal was returning here to find her when the time came, yet she needed to leave now. There was only one place she could go where she knew Uriah would have to meet with her.

Rahab followed the familiar hallways until she came to the doorway she sought. As she placed her hand on the door knob, her heart began to pound. The memories flooded back to her as if it were yesterday. Her palms grew sweaty and her stomach was almost bursting with butterflies just as it had hundreds of times before.

The Priestess pushed open the door to find the room dimmed by heavy curtains that hung in the windows. *Good*, she thought. *I will have time to prepare.*

****

Nimal knew very few of his men would have survived the raid, yet he made his way to the market place. Adon had arranged for the men to assemble after the attack and toast their success. What a joke that had turned out to be. It was as though the Israelites had known their plans all along and this troubled Nimal. Who had tipped them off? Was it the whore? Her pretty spy; or even worse, one of the royal household?

The Captain sat down heavily on the bench and called the serving girl over for ale. She looked at his soot-covered face and the colour drained from her features. Nimal suddenly realised he had not had the forethought to even clean himself up.

'Fetch me an ale woman, and a cloth. Don't you know a fighting man when you see one?'

The barmaid almost curtsied as she retreated. Nimal wondered over her reaction. He was a returning hero. He had almost conquered the invading horde single handed, almost. He stifled a laugh at his own predicament.

He continued to convince himself of his bravery as the serving girl returned, almost spilling the large stone mug of ale in his lap with the slap he delivered to her butt. 'How about a little snog for a returning hero?' He pulled the squealing young woman into his lap as he took a long swig of his ale.

The girl wriggled and squirmed as the Captain put down his almost empty mug on the table and thrust his hand down the bodice of the girl's top, groping her breast. 'That's it sweetness. What have you got for Nimal now?'

'Another ale Sir!' The girl pushed away from the Captain handing him the wet rag to clean up.

Nimal took the rag, drained his drink and nodded to the barmaid. He loved it when they teased him. It made the conquest all the more rewarding. His head was spinning and the Captain scowled at his stupidity. He had spent the night fighting and exerting himself. The ale had gone straight to his head.

The girl returned with another ale and the Captain used the last of his energy to pull her back onto his lap. He took a huge gulp at his ale, while running his hand up the girl's leg and under her tunic. She struggled more and his excitement grew until a large rough hand landed on his shoulder. 'What is the mcaning of this?' Nimal was agitated now. His groin was just heating up.

'Your presence is requested Nimal. It seems you haven't only pissed off the Royal guard, you have the attention of two of our most esteemed Princes' and that can never be good.'

Nimal tried for another grab at the serving girl as she made her escape. He turned to see the Commander of the Royal guard standing over him, one hand on his hip, drifting absently toward his sword and the other firmly planted on the collar of his tunic.

He considered his options until a quick survey revealed three more guards standing at one end of the tavern, with two more nervously playing with their sword hilts at the other.

'I believe you have a report to offer his Lordship and it better be good.' The Commander continued. 'And Prince Adon had best not take too long in making himself known.' The Commander scanned the tavern, the street and the marketplace nearby as he spoke.

Nimal pondered if now was the time and considered it probably was not. Once word got out about Adon's death, the situation was only going to get more complicated. Instead the Captain of the city guard decided he would talk up his heroics in the hopes of gaining some support.

'Sir, since when has delivering a bloody blow to our enemies been pissing anyone off?' Nimal continued, oblivious to the jerking of his tunic. 'I was following the Lord Adon. What greater deed can a soldier do than following his Prince into battle?'

'He can follow the orders of the reigning Prince, not go off on a mission that has surely sealed the deaths of most of the city, you dumb ass.' Further conversation was abruptly interrupted by additional guards lifting Nimal from his feet and dragging him from the tavern.

The barmaid brushed her skirt back down and winked at the Commander as the Captain of the guard was hauled away, kicking and grumbling. 'Thanks for the heads-up Nora'. The Commander whispered.

'My absolute pleasure Commander.'

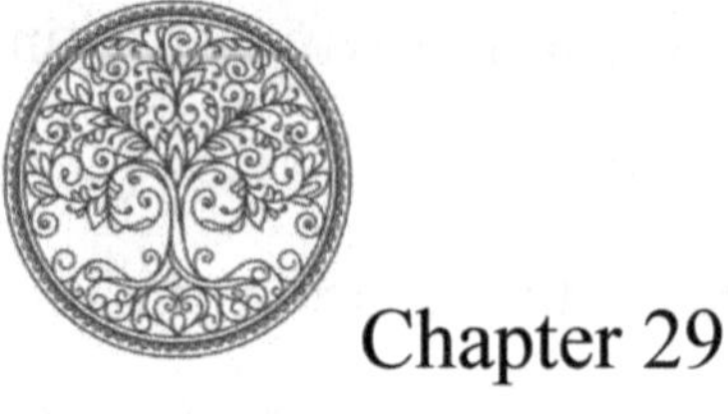

Chapter 29

Salmah had spent much of the morning clearing the bodies of the dead and checking on all the people, their livestock and the provisions. The fires had taken the rest of the night and into the early hours of the morning to get under control. So much devastation lay in the wake of the fire storm that Salmah was struggling to stay strong.

The young leader had thought he had seen the worst until he had found Deshaun's body. The boy he had grown up with, his best friend had taken a throwing knife to his neck and how his body had not been overtaken by the fire, Salmah still did not understand.

At first Salmah had just felt numb. It was as though he had sustained a beating, having all the air knocked from his lungs until there was no way of drawing another breath. His heart was heavy with guilt as he considered his role in this assault. If only he had chased Uriah.

Deshaun had died bravely, doing what he believed in and Salmah could not shake the feeling he lacked the Levite's conviction.

The words had come to his mind, as though they were spoken as a whisper in his ear. Salmah could almost feel the breath of the speaker upon his earlobe. For a moment, he thought the hair on his head had moved with the words and the hairs on his neck stood alert.

You are braver than you believe leader of Judah. Your time is now. Your journey planned, your path set. The Priestess will join you and you will lead your people into true freedom. A freedom the Lord your God has chosen for you.

He was still sitting by Deshaun's lifeless body, lost in his thoughts trying to make sense of the voice in his head when the call came for him to meet with Joshua. There was so much he wanted to ask Joshua but he could not decide where to start.

Was he to return to Jericho and try to make peace with Uriah? He doubted it. Deep down he knew Joshua relished this as fuel for his cause, to bring down the walls and crush the inhabitants of the Canaanite city.

This did not sit well with the leader of Judah and then there was the voice. Was it of the Lord or was it a demon tempting him. *Let your heart guide you Salmah.* The young man looked around for the source. He did not feel fear, only a sense of confusion which was replaced with a feeling of peace that filled his soul to overflowing.

Salmah entered Joshua's tent to see the old man pouring himself a cup of water. He said nothing, only indicated for his spy to take a seat. The silence grew as it appeared to Salmah that Joshua was perpetuating the lack of conversation with a purpose, as though what he wanted to say would be hard.

'I owe you my life Salmah. The Lord shared a vision with you, you are indeed blessed.' Joshua was still confused but he kept his thoughts to himself.

Salmah did not have the heart to tell Joshua that he could not be sure it was God who had spoken to him but he could not refute the fact the vision had saved them all. 'You sound surprised?'

'Indeed. The Priests have assured me it is unprecedented. Only I or they have been privy to such insights in the past.' So why now? He wondered.

Salmah pushed his first response aside. To tell the old man that maybe God thought the Priests and Joshua incapable and unreliable might do more than ruffle a few feathers. 'Interesting.' Was all he could manage to voice.

'It seems the road forward is clear now.' Joshua wasted no time. He put his insecurities aside.

'And what might that entail?' Salmah pushed knowing full well what would come next.

'It seems obvious that the truce you advocated has been rejected by the Lord.'

'That might be one interpretation. Although, if the vision came to me, that might be a contradiction. Surely if my passion for peace was not of God's making, he might not have conveyed His message

through me. Maybe you and the Prophets missed
something!' Salmah knew his logic held no sway with
Joshua and he was still unsure who had warned him
but one thing was certain, Joshua was more rattled
than he revealed.

'Or maybe the attack was a judgement for your
waywardness and the Lord was giving you a lifeline
to return to the fold.'

'You think I have not blamed myself for this!'
Salmah swept his hand around the tent as though he
could see through the walls at the carnage beyond.
'What kind of leader kicks a man when he is down?
What kind of God punishes a servant by killing so
many?' Salmah could feel the knot in his stomach
growing. His anger was barely held in check.

'Careful lad, do not make any rash decisions.'
Joshua spoke as though he were expecting this
conversation.

'I will marry Rahab.'

'I have not given my permission.'

'I do not ask for it Joshua.'

'She must renounce the Goddess Asherah.' Joshua continued as though Salmah had not uttered his revelation.

'I will not enforce that on her. She has risked much to shelter me and used her influence with Uriah to grant me access. The Lord promised her safety. You said so yourself.'

'Safety yes, marriage into the Lord's chosen people He did not. She must renounce Asherah or she cannot join us Salmah.'

Salmah stood to leave. He knew Rahab would never give up her belief in Asherah and how could he ask that of her. He had promised to stay with her not matter what Joshua said. She had warned him that the anointed leader of the Israelites would not accept her. Her prophecy was now fulfilled.

'Think before you go any further boy.' Joshua warned.

'You have made the decision for us Joshua. When the walls fall, the tribe of Judah will part from the remaining tribes. You can grant us lands south of Jericho, to the borders of the Gad and Reuben tribes.'

'You have no idea what you have done Salmah. We have crossed the desert as twelve united tribes.'

'Rubbish. You have threatened multiple tribes including mine exclusion more times than I can count. The Lord has spoken to me Joshua. He shared a vision with me, one that saved many of our people. He is with me and I will take Rahab as my wife and my people will be ruled by you no longer.'

Salmah left the tent without a backward glance.

****

'And you accuse me of meddling!' Asherah spun around to see Moloch behind her, arms crossed and a condescending smile.

'It is not the same and you know it.' She felt like a pouting child when he was around, but she could not contain herself. He brought out the worst in her.

'So you say.' Moloch continued his knowing smile.

'You take lives Moloch. Look around. Look at all these wasted lives. The pain and suffering you have caused.' Asherah was not angry, she was frustrated. Why Yahweh did not intercede was beyond her understanding.

'Your manipulation will take lives Asherah, just not now. What you have instigated amongst the Israelites today will have ramifications that ripple through eternity. The only difference between you and me is you tell yourself lies. You convince yourself that what you do is not meddling with the lives of humanity but that is not true.'

'No Moloch. The difference between you and me is that I do Yahweh's work, not the work of one faction or another.'

'That is if we agree that Yahweh is indeed the creator and that will remain an unprovable theory until all the host of heaven are long gone.'

Asherah drew energy from around her and Moloch smirked knowingly. The sparkling ball of light flew into nothingness as Moloch disappeared. He was infuriating. How could instigating Adon into the violence of firing the encampment be considered equal to what she was doing? He truly was a demon, not a god.

# Chapter 30

Iki was tired. He had very little time before he was expected to meet with Uriah and interrogate the Captain of the guard. He opened the door to his apartment and stumbled as he ducked just in time to avoid a vase to the head.

'What on earth…'

'You had me dressed up like a whore and delivered to your rooms. What were you thinking?'

Realisation struck and Iki smiled. It was not uncommon for him to bring women home to the Palace and his servants had done what they would usually do. They bathed and dressed Nalia and took her to his rooms.

'Wait, wait….' Iki ducked a pillow which was quickly followed by another heavy object that fortunately did not shatter when it hit the floor. 'Stop that. Some of those ornaments you are throwing around are priceless.' Iki knew that was not what

Nalia wanted to hear as soon as the words had left his lips.

'You piece of camel dung. I should have left you tied up in that barn.' Another pillow whirled past Iki's head.

'It is just a misunderstanding. I offered you food and the servants mistook that for something else, obviously.' Iki tried not to smile. The sheer dress Nalia wore was fetching and she was very beautiful without the grime of working in a grotty bar in the soldiers' quarter.

He wisely chose not to bring up the fact that she had originally offered him a complimentary romp in the hay before he became side tracked with his brother.

'Get out, now!' She knelt up on the bed, another pillow in hand and her ample bosom unobscured by the sheer fabric. The light from the window shone from behind her offering an alluring silhouette of her nether region which was quite distracting for the Prince.

'Look, this is my apartment and you are welcome to leave but I need a wash and I have a meeting with the ah.. King.' Iki suddenly remembered his brother might be in charge, but everyone thought his father still was.

'I am not going anywhere. *You* owe me *Prince.*'

'Well if you are not going anywhere, can you please put on some more clothing? There is a robe in my closet over there.' Iki pointed toward the other side of the room. 'That outfit really is very distracting.'

Nalia looked down at her attire and suddenly realised she had forgotten what she was wearing. 'Turn around!' she demanded.

Iki begun to turn his back. 'You do remember you offered yourself to me only last night.' Another pillow struck the back of his head and he was thankful Nalia had not tossed another hard object. He knew she was not really that mad with him, but he appreciated her playing hard to get. In truth, the chase was far more fun than the catch and he was enjoying the game.

He had known the moment he met Nalia she was different and it was confirmed when she had helped release him and then followed him to the Palace. She could have left him tied up in the barn. She could have left after he was freed and ignored his predicament but she had come with him. Nalia was right, he owed her and he always repaid his debts. That was a debt he was looking forward to making good on.

****

Danal had watched Rahab leave the King's apartment. She had been on her way to tell the Priestess that Uriah had arrived back in the Palace. She could not explain exactly why but she had followed at a distance, wondering where Rahab was going.

It did not take long to realise her destination. Rahab had knocked on Uriah's door and when no one had answered, she had entered. Danal was not afraid of what Rahab might do to the Prince, she was more afraid of what Uriah would do to Rahab.

Danal longed for Uriah to want her but she knew he never would. He loved Rahab with every fibre of his being and the fact he had never offered to marry her after Rahab opened her establishment confirmed his feelings.

Her very best friend held the heart of the man she adored firmly in her grasp but had no idea and no inclination to do anything about it. Rahab would never be Uriah's, making sure he could never truly be hers. Even if he did marry her out of some sense of duty, his heart belonged to the Priestess.

Danal had never felt more powerless. Should she stop Rahab from going to his room? Should she tell him Rahab is there? Should she simply give up and accept Iki's advances even though she knew Iki would not marry her either?

Her decision was made for her; Uriah came down the opposite end of the hallway heading straight for his rooms. Danal turned and quickly moved out of sight.

****

Rahab scanned the room looking for somewhere other than the bed to sit. She wondered how on earth Uriah did not possess a desk and chair in his apartment. The room was sparser than the Priestess remembered and she had been there often in her younger years.

She sat on the bed after a few moments, realising there was nowhere else. She was lost in thought, recalling memories that heated her heart among other places. She felt guilty recalling their many nights of passion. Salmah could be hurt or worse.

She could not deny that she still found Uriah attractive. They had history and a lot of it but he had made his choice many years ago and being a Prince of Jericho was more important than her.

The door rattled and Rahab fought the urge to preen herself. 'Stupid woman' she grumbled under her breath as her cheeks flushed ever so slightly.

Uriah froze as he entered his room. His mind raced as he took in the scene. Rahab was sitting on his bed, a flush of colour on her cheeks he had not seen for more years than he cared to recall. He moved the short distance from the door to the edge of the bed. His heart almost skipped a beat as she spoke.

'Uriah. We need to talk.' Rahab stood from the bed inadvertently coming into Uriah's embrace. The Prince reached out absently touching her hair and Rahab took his hand in hers. 'Really Uriah. We have to talk.'

'I have missed you Rahab.' Uriah managed huskily. 'I have wanted to speak with you too.' The Prince moved in to kiss Rahab and she stepped back, releasing her grip on his hand. The act took more determination than the Priestess expected but she forced herself to stay the course. She had too much to do and then there was Salmah.

Uriah's mind returned to the present as the reality of Rahab's actions struck home. 'You come to my rooms uninvited Rahab. What am I to think?' The words were spoken softly, almost painfully and Rahab suppressed the urge to reach out to her past lover.

'I did not wish to lead you on Uriah. I simply was not sure you would meet with me after everything.'

Uriah thought about his answer. Should he tell her everything? Would she agree to marry him after everything they had been through? 'You know I will always receive you Rahab. We have known each other too long but you are right, it has been a long night.'

Rahab looked into Uriah's eyes and saw the anguish. Where to begin she wondered, 'I think the Physician has tried to poison your father, or at the very least he has hidden the attempts from you.'

'How on earth would you know?' The mood was broken at last and Uriah visibly pulled himself up as he stepped away from Rahab toward his wash basin.

'I visited Hamilkot while I waited for you. I had a feeling, a premonition if you like and when I got there Malic was so nervous. He was agitated and sweating and when I tried to examine your father he became even more anxious and called for the guards.'

Rahab saw Uriah brace to complain. 'Before you complain, I got a look at his eyes.'

'What does that mean?' Uriah shrugged and Rahab opened her hands as though he should know what she was talking about.

'Has it been that long that you do not recall my skills at healing?' Rahab hid the sadness and continued. 'The white of his eyes were yellow and the irises were faded.'

'We know he has been unwell and the Physician has not been able to tell us why. The colour of his eyes changing is likely nothing new.'

'If only it were that simple. The yellowing of his eye is from his liver failing to process a foreign chemical in his blood; likely poison. The sudden lightening of the colour of the iris is usually indicative of an infection; a side-effect to his poisoning.'

Uriah processed the information slowly and eventually he nodded his understanding. No matter their history, the Prince knew he could trust Rahab's judgement. 'I will send for the Physician as soon as I interrogate a prisoner. You say father is recovering now and not in immediate danger?' Rahab nodded. 'Good. I will clean up and then you can come with me. I have an old friend I think you will enjoy getting reacquainted with.

 Chapter 31

Salmah's adrenalin was firing as he packed his bag. He wanted to return to Jericho and never come back to the encampment but he knew that when the time came to raze the walls of Jericho, he would need to stand with his people.

He could hardly believe his eyes as he left the charred remnants behind. The Priests and soldiers had rallied together with trumpets and spears to march around the city of Jericho once more. It was not first light as it had been each morning before today, but it was a show of conviction Salmah could not help but feel proud of.

A sense of urgency dug like a knife into Salmah's heart as the sight reminded the tribesman of how little time they had left. With less than two days remaining before the trumpets would sound one final time, Salmah could only hope Rahab had begun gathering her family to her.

Salmah pondered if climbing the walls was wise in full daylight. He had always returned under the cover of darkness but that was not an option today. It would be hours before sunset and he needed to return to Rahab, find Uriah and intercede to avoid a slaughter he knew would be difficult to prevent.

As he began the climb he considered the events to this point. Who had warned him? Who had guided him to Rahab? There were those amongst every nation who thought belief in a higher power to be nothing more than superstition. In truth, if he had not seen what he had, he might well have been one such man.

Now he had witnessed the crossing of the Jordan. He had *accidentally* found his way into the home of Rahab who protected Deshaun and himself even at risk of her own life. He had heard the voice of whoever warn him about the attack that could have killed many of his people. No, there was someone or something guiding his steps. He could feel it.

Some people believed you were either lucky or you were not. Others believed you made your own life, but when Salmah thought of the wonder of life, he felt this explanation lacking.

How is a baby grown within its mother? How does the plant grow from a seed and reproduce more seed at the perfect time to reproduce another plant again and again? The wonder of nature was too amazing to call an accident, or luck.

No, there were no accidents, no coincidence in life. There was a master in charge of the plan, even if he could not see or feel him all the time.

Exactly who that master was, Salmah was beginning to wonder. Was it the God of Israel or was it Asherah the Goddess of the Canaanites?

Joshua always claimed the God of the Israelites had forbidden the worship of other gods, back when the slaves escaped from Egypt. He often told the story of when the people had grown bored and disillusioned as they waited for the prophet to return with the law of Israel; the very same laws that were written on the tablets of stone and were said to reside in the Covenant of God that the Priests now paraded around the walls of Jericho.

While the people had waited many days for the Prophet to return, they had built a golden statue of the demon Baal. The Prophet had been furious, but Salmah often wondered why. The people had not known they were not to worship other gods until the Prophet returned with the laws. Either way, the point was that the God of Israel acknowledged that other gods existed. So why was one god more righteous than the other?

Salmah reached the top of the rope and threw his legs up into the window of Rahab's washroom. Musaf jumped at the noise and rushed around the corner, meat cleaver in hand.

'Ah, it is you.' He grunted and returned to his work without another word.

Salmah walked to the washroom doorway and peered into the dining area. 'Where is Rahab?' He continued to survey the patrons and staff.

'With Uriah.'

'Really, that is all you have for me? With Uriah, why?'

'How should I know?' The cook shrugged his enormous shoulders causing the tattoos on his biceps to ripple with the movement. 'She sent word this morning that she would not be in to work. She left before dawn, after the fires. The rest you will have to ask her.'

Salmah frowned. The dining room was full of soldiers from the Royal guard. He was known to most of them and he could not be sure if he would be received amicably or not after last night. He needed to get to Uriah, but how?

'Any chance of sneaking me out of here?'

Musaf raised his eyebrows, thought for a moment until a wicked grin crossed his face. 'I can think of only one possible option. Shiba!' The cook pushed Salmah out of sight and leaned out into the dining hall as he called for the young Priestess.

Shiba quietly apologised to her guest and stood to leave. The soldier complained until another Priestess took the acting hostess's place by sitting upon the disgruntled man's lap. Thoughts of Shiba were quickly forgotten. The priestess smiled politely and made her way to the washroom.

'So quickly I am replaced.' She grinned at Musaf. 'What do you need? I was looking forward to that one's tip.' The Priestess indicated with her head as she spoke.

'I have a far more pressing role for you.' Musaf still wore the unnerving grin and Salmah could not help but squirm a little. 'This one wants to leave unnoticed.' Musaf chuckled. 'Do you think Maurette has anything big enough we can squeeze him into?'

Realisation struck and Salmah backed away into the rear of the washroom, trying desperately to climb the ladder to Rahab's loft as Shiba took on the look of a lioness about to stalk her prey.

'Without a doubt. I am sure we can manage something.'

****

Salmah tried to leave as discretely as he could. It had taken far too long and the excessive rouge made the tribesman's face feel like he had a mud mask on. As he moved his cheeks he could have sworn the clay based *foundation* Shiba had used, was in fact creating crazy cracks that would be sure to draw unwanted attention.

He was almost to the door when an inebriated soldier pinched his backside. He yelped, swung around to punch the man before he realised what he was doing. Shiba stepped in between the two of them, a smile upon her face she could not contain.

'Jacko, come with me. This one is a little plump for you.'

'No, no,' the man staggered. 'I like a bit of meat….,' belch, 'on the bone Shiba.' Another belch. 'Can I have…,' a deep breath, 'this one?'

Fortunately for Salmah the man was so drunk he could barely stand. Shiba took the man's hand, steering him away from the petrified spy. 'Maurette. I think this one is for you.' Shiba winked at Salmah who mouthed the words. 'I owe you one.' as he slipped out of the Inn into the busy market square beyond.

Thankfully Maurette's dress had covered Salmah's regular clothing. He ducked into the alley by the Inn and discarded the outfit. He wiped his face with the dress, spitting on the fabric for added moisture. He was sure he had not removed it all and no doubt looked like a performing juggler from the town square, but he had to get to the Palace, now!

Chapter 32

Rahab had watched Uriah take off his tunic and bathe his chest and face at the basin. It was unnerving to be in his room. She had promised herself to Salmah, but the Prince and she shared so much history and he was half naked. The Priestess was finding it difficult to focus.

'That should do it.' Uriah collected a clean tunic from his side table and pulled it on over his head. He tied it at the waist with a thick leather belt and Rahab watched as he brushed his leather riding pants down with his still moist palms. He quickly rinsed and dried his hands before turning to the Priestess.

'What do you think? Do I pass for King in this outfit?' Uriah smiled, his good humour returning.

'You have always been fit to be King Uriah. Jericho could not have a better man for the job.'

'They could have my father back on his feet. He would have handled this so much more efficiently.'

'No, he would have done exactly what the men did last night and you know it. You are leading now for a reason. Trust me on this.' Rahab walked up to the Prince and gently kissed him on the cheek. 'Do not underestimate yourself Prince. The Goddess is watching.'

Uriah frowned as Rahab turned to leave. He was confused. Not only about the Goddess watching over him, but of the tenderness of Rahab's kiss. Why were women so damned confusing? Should he say something? His chance was lost as Rahab opened the door to the hallway.

'Oh, Rahab. I did not know you were *here,*' Danal lied.

Rahab knew it looked awkward and she suddenly felt uncomfortable. 'I, ah, needed to tell Uriah about his father.' Rahab turned to Uriah for support. She frowned and indicated with her eyes for him to say something, but he had no idea what she wanted from him. Men could be so stupid she thought. Danal was going to believe the worst.

'Iki is ready and sent me to fetch Uriah.' Danal did not wait for further information. She turned and headed down the hall toward the King's meeting chambers.

Rahab turned on Uriah. 'For the sake of Asherah, why did you say nothing?' Rahab stormed off leaving Uriah open mouthed and more confused than he thought possible.

****

Uriah followed Rahab into the large meeting hall. Iki sat upon the smaller lounging area with a woman Uriah had never seen before. Just like Iki to bring one of his female companions to an interrogation of a rebel soldier.

For the first time since last night he wondered over Adon. He could only hope that Rahab's Goddess was watching over all his family, not only himself.

'Iki, I see you have company.' Uriah frowned his disapproval and the woman replied with a sneer that could strip the skin like acid.

'Uriah. I would not have raised the alarm without Nalia's help. She is my guest.'

'Well maybe your guest would be more comfortable in your private quarters.' Uriah could not be sure but for a moment he thought the woman might actually have growled.

'Ah brother. I see you have some unconventional company of your own.' Iki stood and took a few steps down from the dais to greet Rahab. 'You are looking as beautiful as even Priestess.'

'And you also Iki.' Rahab smiled at the stare she received from the young woman. She could see the girl had spunk but she needed to learn when to keep it hidden; something Rahab realised she was yet to master herself. The thought only served to widen the Priestesses smile which lead to even more agitation for the girl. 'My name is Rahab, Nalia. It is lovely to meet you.'

'Alright, alright. Are the pleasantries out of the way now! Can we get on with what we came to do?' Uriah was growing frustrated with the façade.

Rahab looked at Danal who had not said a word and wondered what she was thinking: two Princes with two 'scarlet' women joining what would be a rather unconventional conversation about traitors and threats of magic from the Israelites.

Now all that was missing was a spy. Rahab smiled quietly to herself but as she thought of Salmah she felt guilty once more. Was he safe? How could she have lusted over Uriah as she had? Was she really worthy of a man like Salmah who had done nothing but put his people and even her own people first?

'Bring in the prisoner Commander.' Uriah frowned at his brother taking control of the meeting. 'What? I have a little score to settle. It is because of this man that I got tied up in a barn for hours.'

Rahab almost gasped as Nimal entered, escorted by two large Royal Guards. She forced herself to remain calm and wait to see what was going on.

Nimal puffed up his chest as though he were walking the streets of the city, enforcing the law once more.

'Tell us about the raid on the Israelites Nimal and do not leave out a single detail.' The Captain had barely reached the foot of the dais before the Prince spoke. There was no doubt Uriah meant business.

The Captain of the city guard squared his shoulder on the acting King. 'The Prince wanted men, brave men and I supplied them Sir. There is not much more to say.'

'Of course there is more to say you imbecile. Did you really think that Adon acted on the King's orders when he had me tied up and incapacitated?' Iki pointed at the Captain as he spat the words out.

'The King is not ruling here though is he!' It was not a question and Iki looked at Uriah for confirmation.

'Who told you that?' Uriah lent forward menacingly.

'The Prince Sir. He told us that King Hamilkot would have slaughtered those invaders and that you were sitting on your hands, playing *Nice Prince* instead of wiping their faces in the mud. That's what he said Sir.'

'Your words border on rebellion.' Rahab spoke for the first time.

'That's a matter of perspective. You're the whore who harboured the spies.'

'Watch your mouth Nimal.' Uriah warned.

'What, she won't let you bone her anymore. Are you hoping if you play nice with her, she will open her legs for you again?'

Uriah's knuckles were white as he gripped his sword hilt. 'You really are scum Nimal. You think everything revolves around fighting and rutting but that is the work of a weak mind.

'Then your brother was famous for his weak mind.'

It took a moment for the Captain's words to sink in. 'Was!' Uriah drew his sword to the man's throat as the Royal guard all placed their hands on their sword hilts. Uriah held out his free hand for them to remain calm.

Nimal swallowed hard. How had he let that slip? There was no going back now. 'It was his choice Sir. He wanted to bloody their noses. He wanted to see them suffer. We thought that if we attacked before they did, then the walls would not come down. The city would be safe. It would have worked except no reinforcements came. You blasted cowards just stood and watched.'

There was an uncomfortable silence. Uriah still held his sword at the man's throat and a trickle of blood had formed at the point. Rahab stood and placed her hand on the hilt of the Prince's sword, gently pushing it down and away from the Captain. 'I think he is not worth it Uriah. Besides, you need to know more.'

The vein in Uriah's forehead was pulsing as he took a deep breath, sheathing his sword. Guilt flooded his thoughts. He could have sent more men but he did not and now he needed to know the truth of it. 'You did not answer the question. Where is Adon?'

'He didn't make it.'

'Who killed him?'

'You need to let me in man. I need to see Uriah and the Priestess.' A servant was pushing a man away from the doorway as the Commander drew his sword. Rahab saw Salmah push past the servant.

'It is alright Commander. He is with me.' The Commander sheathed his sword and stepped back, allowing Salmah to pass.

Uriah ignored the interruption and pushed the Captain for more. 'You did not answer my question, who killed my brother?' Nimal looked straight at Salmah and Uriah followed his gaze.

'I did Uriah. I am sorry but it was me.'

The silence grew but Nimal recovered almost immediately. 'And you call me a traitor. You leave your brother to die unaided and he, the spy with the Whore kills him. Hah!'

The Commander drew his sword and his men followed. Rahab screamed at Uriah who pushed her aside, knocking her to the ground heavily. Danal ran to aid Rahab, while Iki's face grew paler.

Salmah held up his hands in surrender. The Commander reached the spy first, hitting him in the face with the reversed hilt of his sword and elbow.

Rahab cried out. Her head was bleeding and the room was spinning out of control. The last thing she heard was Danal and Salmah calling her name.

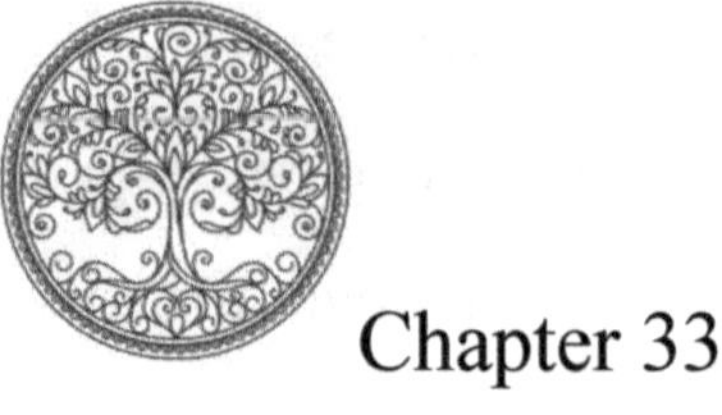

Chapter 33

Rahab felt heavy as though a stone had been tied to her legs before being tossed into a well of cold water. She gasped for air but each time she reached the surface, her lungs filled with water.

She could hear voices, calling her name but when she tried to speak, no sound left her lips.

'We need to call the Physician.' Danal sounded frightened.

'We cannot. It is complicated Danal.' That was Uriah. Where was Salmah? Then she remembered. *Oh Goddess. Please help me.*

The darkness faded and Rahab found herself in a beautiful garden, surrounded by brightly coloured flowers with a stream of crystal clear water running through the centre. There were waterfalls running from the sky into the pond from all directions and the Priestess became lost in the splendour.

'You cannot stay long child. So much depends on you.' The woman had golden hair and her dress floated as though a strong wind blew all around, but Rahab felt nothing.

'Who are you?' Where am I? Rahab continued to look around, like a child on her first visit to the market square. So much colour, so many sounds, so much light it was intoxicating.

'You have heard my voice child, but now you can see me.' Rahab frowned until the truth struck her. 'Yes Rahab. My name is Asherah and this is my temple. Walk with me.' The Goddess held out her hand and Rahab floated to her feet. The Priestess felt as though she were walking on silk cushions. The ground gave way ever so slightly with each step she took. The sensation made her giggle and the Goddess smiled warmly at her obvious joy.

'Your temple is amazing. Where is it?'

'That is my secret Rahab for if everyone knew where I took my rest I would never find the peace I need to regenerate my own powers.'

Rahab's mind wandered as she took in the brightly coloured birds, the sky that never ended and the water falls that sprang from nowhere. A thought came to her suddenly. A sensation of fear, but why would anyone be afraid in this place.

Salmah. Where is Salmah? She gasped. 'Oh Goddess, why? Why did Salmah kill Adon? Uriah will never come to you now. He will be too enraged to think clearly. What are we to do? I need to save Salmah.'

'There are forces at work that you cannot possibly fight. I have done what I can, but now I need you to focus and help me.'

'Why? You can just appear to Uriah and tell him to stop.'

'No, there are rules. Uriah is not ready. He will not receive me Rahab. He still does not believe. Only you can convince him.'

'I brought Salmah into the Palace. I saved the spy who killed his brother. He is not going to listen to me.'

'You will be surprised what love can do Rahab. It is time to go.'

'But I want to stay! No!'

'Rahab, it is me. Uriah. You were dreaming. We were so worried about you. I am sorry. Hurting you was the last thing I wanted to do.'

'Where is Salmah?' Rahab tried to sit up. She did not see the pain in Uriah's eyes.

'You need rest Priestess. Danal will stay with you.' Uriah stood to leave as Rahab remembered what the Goddess had said.

'Uriah. You have to go to the Shrine of Asherah. You must ask the Goddess for help.'

Uriah patted her hand gently. 'You need your rest. You are still delirious.' The door closed heavily behind the Prince as Rahab drifted back into unconsciousness.

Chapter 34

'What do we do with Nimal?' Iki pulled a large chunk of flat bread from the platter and smeared it with soft goat cheese. The Princes had retreated to the only place that truly offered them comfort. The Palace kitchen was enormous, with long preparation tables, a cook fire on each wall and rows of open cupboards loaded with fresh fruit, vegetables, cured meats and stacks of newly baked bread.

As children, they had taken refuge there whenever trouble brewed: when their father had grumbled at them; when they had argued with each other; When Iki's pet rabbit had died and when Rahab and Uriah had finally given up hope of marrying, this had been their haven.

The copious food provisions, the smell of wood-fired bread, the chatter of the kitchen staff and the head cook who would try to make them eat even more food, claiming they needed more meat on their bones. All the joys of their childhood served to provide some resemblance of clarity for the Princes and today they needed clarity more than ever before.

'What do we do with the spy more to the point?' Uriah refused to use his name. It humanised him and he did not want to feel any sense of pity toward the man who had murdered his brother.

'I think the pressing matter is Nimal. He is out of control.' Iki spoke with a mouthful of food and Uriah had to laugh.

'You never did learn table manners Iki.'

'Better than Adon.' The men smiled until they pondered their loss. 'He was a big idiot Uriah.'

'That he was, but he was our brother.' Uriah took a long gulp of milk, leaving his white moustache in place longer than necessary before wiping it away with the back of his hand. 'We should let Nimal go. You follow him and if he tries to incite anymore stupid raids on the Israelites, I leave it up to you to deal with him. Either way, we will see if he has ties with anyone else in the city that we need to worry about.'

Iki nodded. 'I will take a handful of Royal guards with me. I am not the fighter Adon was, that is obvious after he strung me up like a slaughtered pig.' Uriah laughed.

'You can handle Nimal with no trouble at all brother but just in case, take some additional help. Better safe than sorry.' Uriah grabbed a handful of dried fruit and put them all in his mouth in one swoop. 'I love eating here…' The Prince chewed loudly, 'no airs and graces, no one to watch. It is liberating.' Both men laughed.

'What about Salmah? We need to hear what he has to say about last night. We need the full picture of what happened or we cannot hope to understand what to expect from the invaders if they breach the walls.'

'Yes, I know. They will bring the walls down Iki. I am sure of it. Magic or Miracle. No matter what they call it, those Priests who carry that golden box have skills we cannot hope to match.'

'What of Asherah. Rahab talks about her often. Can she help us?'

'Asherah is a legend brother, something working women invented to legitimise their occupation.'

'That is harsh. I would love to see you repeat that statement to Rahab.' Iki laughed as Uriah squirmed. 'So, no Goddess to help us you say.'

'No Goddess Iki, just a few keen minds. I will think on it, but we need to save our people without letting Adon's death go unpunished. I do not know how to tell Rahab, but her pet spy might have to be the martyr in this unfortunate political climate.

****

Salmah had known hardship in the form of near starvation, but a beating was new to him. He struggled to open both his eyes and his ribs felt like they were going to poke out of his skin each time he moved.

'Killing the Prince was not your best idea spy.' The soldier on guard noticed Salmah was awake.

'Invading our camp and firing the homes of innocent shepherds was not the work of heroes either.' Salmah regretted the words too late. Another kick to his ribs brought a loud crack. Yes, definitely broken.

'I think I am looking forward to your execution. Spies rarely get a trial in Jericho. It is pretty much a done deal.' The guard laughed.

'Do you have children?' Salmah saw the shock on the man's face.

'What is it to you?'

'Nothing really. I was just trying to save them, that is why I was here. I did not have to come back you know. I could have stayed in the camp and watched the funeral pyre happy in the knowledge there was one less Prince in the Palace.' Another kick. *Damn*

'Tell it to the King.'

Salmah was tempted to mention the King was a little out of reach, but his ribs were hurting far too much already. No, he needed to formulate his argument for Uriah. He could only hope the man could see reason, but after the meeting hall, he was less confident.

'Tell me is the Priestess alright?' The guard frowned at the prisoner.

'What's it to you?'

'I saw her head hit the floor when the Prince pushed her. I am simply concerned for her health.'

'None of your business spy. Your time is short, so make the most of it and don't waste your time thinking about things that don't concern you.'

Easy for him to say. He was not in love with the Priestess. He was not the one with his heart in his throat as she landed hard and her head started to bleed. He saw the red drops in her nostrils. *Lord, let Rahab be alright. It is my fault. I fought with Joshua. Punish me, but please spare Rahab.*

****

Danal held Rahab's hand until she was sure the Priestess was sleeping once more. She checked her pulse and changed the moist cloth on her forehead. Uriah had not called the Physician and Danal was worried. She knew there was something he was not telling her, but she had seen enough over the years to know that a head injury needed a cold compress. She only hoped it would be enough.

Rahab was delirious but she had asked for Salmah the moment she awoke. The Priestess was in love with the spy and Danal felt helpless. Uriah loved Rahab, Rahab loved Salmah and she loved Uriah. What a mess. How were any of them to find the happiness they deserved?

Hours passed as Rahab slowly became coherent. They spoke briefly each time she awoke. The Priestess was now resting having fully regained consciousness but drifting in and out of sleep. Danal knew not to let her sleep too long. Every so often she would shake Rahab and force her awake to speak.

'There was nothing…. to it.' Rahab slurred.

'Nothing to what Rahab?' Danal asked, not really caring what she was saying only ensuring she spoke each time she woke up.

'Uriah and me.'

'It is alright Rahab. You can talk when you are fully awake.'

'No, Salmah! Help Salmah!' Rahab slipped back into a deep sleep.

How could she help the spy? Danal considered her options. Breaking him out was impossible, besides there was only so much she was willing to risk for

Rahab and her future with Uriah was not something she was open to losing.

She had never seen Uriah so angry. It was so out of character for him. Maybe she could ask the Physician for a calming draft, or maybe not. If Uriah found out she had spoken with the Physician, it would likely just aggravate him further. He had been very clear on that issue.

Danal called for a servant to stay with Rahab. It was best she speak with Uriah about the Physician and about his temper. Rahab was right, she had stayed passive for too long. She needed to take charge if she wanted to be Uriah's wife she needed to prove to the future King that she would make the perfect Queen.

Chapter 35

Iki was careful. He doubted Nimal had Adon's skill and would likely not see his surveillance, but as Uriah had said, better safe than sorry. The Royal guard were keeping their distance but they were within calling distance should Iki need them.

Nimal had gathered a group around him. The Prince had made it perfectly clear that if he did not keep a low profile until after the siege was over that there would be consequences.

The Captain had told them all about Adon's plans. How it had taken days to get all the supplies together? He retold the story about the attack and firing of the Israelite camp. Nimal shared Adon's last moments including a rather strange account of Adon losing his weapon and the spy killing him in cold blood.

Something about the story just did not sit well with Iki. At the time, he and Uriah had been too enraged to see clearly but as Iki went over the story in his head he knew it unlikely Adon would have lost his weapon and if he had, he would have tried to tear the spy apart with his bare hands. No, Nimal was lying which meant he was up to something.

Iki called a barmaid over with the wave of his hand. He ordered a cup of thick black coffee. The liquid tasted foul without honey, so he sent the barmaid back for a pot of the amber fluid. He needed his wits about him and coffee had a fabulous way of keeping a man's senses alert.

'Do you reckon it's true Sir?' Iki looked at the barmaid who almost whispered the questions.

'Do I think what is true?'

'The King is dead and the Princes are keeping it a secret.' The girl obviously had no idea who she was talking to. Iki had gone to great lengths to disguise himself as a merchant after realising Nalia had recognised him so easily.

'Where did you hear that nonsense?' Iki chuckled to hide his concern.

'Them men over there.' The girl nodded towards Nimal with her head. 'They've been chatting about it for the last hour. Mia heard them and then she told Becca, who works for the baker and Becca just told me.'

'I am sure it is mere gossip. If the King were dead, then the Prince would have already been crowned. There is no real point in hiding it from the people, is there now!'

The barmaid frowned. 'That kinda makes sense. I guess.' The girl scuttled off to continue her duties.

Iki considered sorting the mess out right there and then, but he wanted to know more and the only way he was going to discover what Nimal was truly up to was to wait and see. The former Captain of the guard dispersed his group of men and Iki watched them all speak to anyone who would listen as they left the tavern and made their way into the market square.

Unrest and uncertainty were bound to create fear. Nimal wanted to generate enough anxiety within Jericho that when the time came, the people would fight, not accept the Israelites into the city. Any chance of Uriah finding a peaceful resolution was diminishing by the second and Iki could not decide what he should do about it.

Nimal left the tavern and headed for the back streets. Iki followed at a discreet distance.

****

Danal spotted Uriah as he made his way to the dungeon. She took a deep breath, smoothed her dress and adjusted her hair before calling out.

'Uriah. May I join you?'

'The dungeon is no place for a woman Danal.' The Prince barely turned to acknowledge her approach. Danal calmed her nerves.

'I doubt you would say that to Rahab.'

Uriah stopped with his back still facing Danal. She studied his posture, trying to decide if she had added to his anger. Uriah was growing prone to outbursts since hearing of Adon's death. She knew he had been on edge.

'True.' Uriah turned around in the corridor and waited for Danal to catch up. 'Why do you want to come?'

Danal considered her answer carefully. 'Rahab cannot be here.' She knew there was more she wanted to say but could not be sure Uriah was ready to hear it. She felt braver than she had ever felt before but that was not enough, not yet.

Uriah looked unsatisfied with her answer but did not press her. 'It is not going to be pretty Danal. I am fairly sure the guards will have taken it upon themselves to dish out a little old fashioned justice on the spy.'

'I am stronger than you think Uriah.' Danal placed her hand on Uriah's allowing him to guide her down the stone stairs into the darkness of the lower levels of the Palace. As children Danal and the Princes had played in the dungeon amongst the catacombs of tombs, artefacts and cells that were rarely used.

Jericho had long ago abandoned the system of imprisoning men. Instead they put those who committed crimes against their society to work within the city. The young and healthy built bridges, paved roadways, constructed buildings around the Palace and training ground while those too old or young to take on heavy labour were given gardening, landscaping, harvesting or other menial work. If their crimes were minor, they could earn their freedom and many did.

Long term detention was uncommon and even if the prisoners were working as slaves for the rest of their natural life, they were guarded in small groups and camped around the city in stables and other outbuildings. The dungeon was reserved for only the most prestigious of prisoners; those like Salmah who were imprisoned for political reasons.

The smell of stale sweat and urine drifted to Danal and she could not help but wonder why she had never noticed the odour as a child. Uriah patted her hand and Danal realised she had unconsciously squeezed the Prince's arm as the darkness closed in around her. There was a light in the tunnel below and the soft glow reached her eyes which slowly adjusted to the dimness.

A short walk brought them to the first of the cells. 'How goes it Keret?' Uriah patted the guard on the shoulder as he approached.

'We have been having a perfectly wonderful time Sir.'

Uriah studied Salmah. He was doubled over at the rear of the cell, his eyes closed but not by choice. He held his head high, trying to see through swollen slits, yet taking in every word, alert and unbroken.

'Leave us for a moment Keret.' The guard shrugged as though the Prince was making a mistake but did not argue. He stepped away from the outside of the cell and took a short stroll, just far enough away to not hear, but close enough to bring his sword to bear should it be necessary.

'You put on quite a show of genuine support spy.' Uriah paced the outside of the cell, his hands clasped behind his back like his father used to do. Salmah said nothing; instead, he rolled over to face the rear of his cell, turning his back on Uriah.

Danal saw Uriah clench his fists and knew now was the time to say something. 'Salmah, tell me what really happened.' Uriah frowned and made to protest, yet Danal lifted a hand in the air stopping the words before they left his lips. 'I have heard so much about you. Most of it so positive, and then there is the story our wayward guard has told us last night. Truly, I want no more than to know your side of the story.'

Uriah continued to pace. He had no idea why he had allowed Danal to continue speaking, but the spy was responding to her technique and it seemed obvious from the wounds he had sustained that force was not yielding any reward.

Salmah groaned as he forced himself to a sitting position. 'Nothing I say will undo what has been done.'

'There is truth in that, but what you say may prevent further misfortune.' Danal moved closer to the cell and Uriah reached out, grabbing her arm firmly. She smoothed his rough hand with gentle strokes and smiled reassuringly. She was sure her face betrayed her concern, but Uriah appeared to relax at the touch.

'Adon came for Joshua, our leader. I had a dream and we were more prepared than we should have been. I begged him to lay down his weapon, to return to the city but he had a madness in his eyes I have never seen before.'

Uriah recalled Iki's similar description after his unfortunate run-in with Adon. He wanted to hate this man. He wanted to avenge his brother's death but Iki had said he did not trust Nimal and Uriah shared his brother's reservations.

'It is still my fault. I take full responsibility. I should have insisted on the Prince's answer to Joshua's terms. I should have returned to my encampment the day before to deliver the message and none of this would have happened.'

'That is not entirely true.' Uriah moved forward. 'Adon was headstrong and stubborn. I should have seen this coming. Is there any chance Joshua will still offer our people safe passage?'

Salmah hung his head. 'I wish I could confidently say yes, but Joshua was only humouring my leadership of the Judah people when he considered sparing lives. He will kill every able-bodied man he sees when the walls come down.'

'What if I offer him my life? Will he spare my people then?'

'No Uriah.' Danal pleaded. 'That will not do.'

'It makes perfect sense. The break of the agreement happened under my leadership. The attack on the Israelites was my fault. Father will recover soon and if he does not, Iki can rule in my place.'

Chapter 36

Salmah was not allowed time to visit Rahab before he left, but Danal had assured him she was recovering well. There was no sneaking beyond the walls of Jericho this day. As the sun broke and the parade of men, trumpets and the Ark of God circled the city walls, Salmah was lowered by rope to the ground below.

As though the earth itself had been waiting for his feet to fall upon it, the ground began to shake. Cracks appeared in the city walls as lumps of stone fell from above, landing randomly. Bystanders who had come to the wall to see what was now a ritual march around the city were frightened by the shaking earth and ran for cover. The shouts of soldiers from above drifted like the dust that was raised by the falling debris.

This was God's last warning. Tomorrow morning, as the sun rose over the hillside, Jericho would fall and who survived depended on one man and that man was a stubborn old fool who was unlikely to listen to one young tribal leader such as he.

He hoped he was wrong about Joshua, but he was also unsure of the outcome he prayed for. On one hand if Joshua did not agree, Uriah would survive and he liked Uriah. He was full of courage, honesty, guile, resourcefulness and had proven to be a great leader.

On the other hand, if Joshua agreed, thousands of the inhabitants of Jericho would live. Uriah would die, but if Iki or his father ruled well, the Israelites and Canaanites could share the lands beyond and prosper. Accepting his people as refugees was all Salmah had ever hoped for. Surely war and death was avoidable? He hoped so.

****

'What do you mean?' Rahab sat up in bed, tossing the soft coverlet to the floor. For the first time, she realised it was Uriah's room she had been sleeping in and wondered where the Prince had stayed.

'Stay right where you are Rahab. You are not yet fully recovered.'

'What was that bull-headed idiot thinking?' Rahab ignored Danal and slid from the warm bed. 'Get my clothes. Where is my tunic?'

'Oh for the love of the Goddess. You are such a stubborn woman.' Danal wrapped her arm around Rahab's waist and placed the Priestesses arm over her shoulder. 'If you insist, at least let me help you.'

Rahab hobbled to the chair where Danal pointed. 'Why did you let him make such a stupid promise?'

'And I have the power of persuasion over Uriah. Yes, of course I can stop the Prince of Jericho making plans to save his people.' Danal did not attempt to keep the mocking tone from her words.

Rahab shook her head. 'So where is Salmah?'

'Taking the message to the leader of the Israelites. Joshua I think he called him.'

'Damn it.' Rahab continued to dress. 'I must see Uriah. I have an important message for him. Why on earth did you take so long to tell me?'

'Oh, I have no idea. No, wait. You were barely conscious. I remember now.' Danal slapped her forehead for added emphasis.

'Alright, alright. I get the point.' Rahab knew she was being unreasonable, but she was frantic. Uriah had to leave with the King. Asherah had been so clear. The Priestess did not understand the prophecy the Goddess spoke of in her dream, but she knew it was important.

Then there was Salmah, gone again and although she knew he was safe, she had not seen him with her own eyes. The story of his beating left a cold feeling in Rahab's stomach and she longed to hold him, bathe his wounds and kiss him back to full strength.

Instead, the walls had shaken and there was no doubt, tomorrow might take the life of any or all those she loved.

****

'So where did he go after the market square?' Uriah sat on the edge of his seat. 'And who is watching him now?'

'The Commander has two men following him while I report to you. He had men whipping up fear all over the city and when the walls shook this morning, there was pandemonium.'

'That is not good. Where is he now?'

'He has found favour with a number of father's council. Apparently with father otherwise occupied, there are a few less than loyal men of politics ready to incite a civil war.'

'Surely this morning's display has them ready to change their minds?'

'You would hope so, but Nimal can be very persuasive. What do you want me to do?

'Take the Commander, at least ten of his best and drag that weasel kicking and screaming through the city streets. I want everyone to see we know what he is up to and we do not approve.'

'Are you sure brother? I was thinking something a little more discrete. Let us not make a martyr of him. The people are scared, if we drag him out publically, he will cry out that we are hiding something,' Iki had an almost mischievous smile on his face. 'which we are of course.'

'Alright, what do you suggest?' Uriah collected a handful of grapes as he sat back to listen.

'Trust me brother. Nimal has two weaknesses other than his stupidity and I know just the person who can exploit both.'

'Uriah. We need to speak.' Rahab entered the meeting hall, flanked by Danal who continued to support the Priestess with one arm wrapped tightly around her waist.

'I am so glad to see you up and about Rahab. I am sorry. I should never have pushed you like that.' Uriah was on his feet, tossing his uneaten grapes back on the low wooden table and leaping from the dais to the ground in one easy jump. 'Here, let me help you.'

'Stop it. All of you. It was just a bump on the head.' Rahab shook her hands frantically, forcing her companions away. 'I need some space.'

Danal and Uriah let go of the Priestess but hovered close by as she made her way up the two steps to the cushions.

Iki stood as the Priestess took her seat. 'What have I missed?' Rahab directed her question to no one in particular.

'Nimal is inciting a riot.' Iki beamed.

'Nothing unexpected about that. What are you doing about it?'

'Well it just so happens Iki might have a plan.' Uriah sat next to Rahab, while Danal walked to the other side of the seating and sat opposite, trying not to concern herself with Uriah's attentiveness towards Rahab.

'I do have a plan and I need your help Rahab, well not your help exactly but possibly Shiba's or is Nimal more of a Maurette type of man?' Rahab smiled as Iki outlined his plan.

'What do you intend doing with him once you capture him?' Rahab had an idea of her own and Nimal might prove to be the perfect distraction. She was unsure if Salmah would consider it righteous, but at this point she was willing to do anything to ensure Asherah got what she wanted and Uriah survived.

Chapter 37

'I did not expect to see you again so soon Salmah.' Joshua watched the leader of Judah carefully, choosing to ignore his obvious wounds.

'The Prince did not take too kindly to the news I killed his brother. Having said that, we came to an arrangement.'

'What arrangement?'

'He wished to convey that his brother's actions were not of his making. He has offered our people asylum in Jericho if you will promise not to kill anyone when the walls come down.'

Joshua thought for a moment, picking up a cup of water and sipping quietly. He studied Salmah's wounds and frowned at some internal conflict.

'I do not believe you understand why we invade Jericho Salmah. It is not for a peaceful settlement.'

'But just because God promised us the land does not mean we have to take it by force.' Salmah allowed his agitation to grow. 'Surely our God is merciful. Surely a peaceful resolution is the best option.'

Salmah knew Uriah had offered his own life in return for the safety of his people, but the Tribesman prayed Joshua would accept a peaceful resolution without the Prince's sacrifice.

'God is merciful to those who love Him Salmah, not to pagans who worship forbidden gods.'

Salmah shook his head. 'Uriah has offered his own life in exchange for you allowing his people to live. He said he will surrender himself and open the gates for you to pass through Jericho into Canaanite lands. He has offered land for our people to settle and farm. He has offered a peaceful future for our children. What more can we want?'

'Uriah will die. We will enslave every man, woman and child in Jericho. They turned from the Lord our God back in the times of Abraham. Their time is done Salmah.'

'No. I gave my word Joshua.' Salmah stood to leave. He needed to warn Uriah.

'You had no right. I speak for our people not you Salmah.' Salmah ignored Joshua and pushed the tent flap open to leave only to find a spear point aimed at his chest. 'I cannot depose you as the leader of your tribe, but you will not leave until the walls fall tomorrow. As you have already promised, after tomorrow we part ways Salmah for you have lost your way and the Priestess of Asherah has tainted you.'

'Or maybe power has tainted you old man? If you believe our Lord wants you to do his dirty work for him. how powerless do you think he is?'

'I will not debate with you Salmah. The walls *will* fall. That is our Lord's doing. Why would he bring down the walls before us, if not to lead us to defeat the Canaanites and enter the Promised Land unencumbered?'

'That sounds like a debate to me.' Salmah smiled.

'Take him to his quarters. Ensure he does not leave.' Joshua waved his hand at the guard.

The guard pushed Salmah outside. He knew he could escape if he wanted to, but lives would be lost and he had no intention of killing anyone he did not have to. Only time would tell if Joshua and his Priests had interpreted God's will clearly. He felt a knot in the pit of his stomach as he considered such a man continuing to lead the Israelites.

No matter what happened, his people would part ways with Joshua after Jericho. For now, he could only pray Rahab had recovered enough to put some sort of plan in motion herself.

****

Rahab felt the urgency of time slipping away from her. How was she going to help Uriah believe in Asherah? The Goddess had been clear that she could not rescue the Prince if he did not invite the Goddess into his heart.

The Priestess pushed the thought aside. For now, she had to focus on helping Iki capture Nimal. His incarceration was paramount to her plans.

Shiba was the perfect lure to catch such a pig, but Rahab's Inn was not a place Nimal was likely to visit again any time soon. Iki knew the Captain spent many hours drinking in the market place tavern and it was only a matter of time before he frequented again.

Nalia had a friend who worked at the tavern and she made the necessary arrangements for Shiba to be on hand when the time came.

It was essential to ensure Nimal was taken away peacefully and that no one was alerted to his departure. His little gang had aggressively turned the rumour mill and arresting the Captain publically would likely result in rioting.

Iki and Nalia watched the tavern from across the lane. Nalia sat on the Prince's lap so that his face could not be seen. Guards were posted down the alleyway near the barn where Adon had detained Iki.

There was nothing Rahab could do now and she was forced to leave so that she was not accidentally seen. She pushed Uriah out of sight and encouraged him to join her. Finally, they were alone to talk.

'I have an idea.' Rahab considered how she was going to approach the subject.

'It is a good plan. I think Nimal will be in custody in no time.'

'No, that was Iki's plan. Mine you might not find so likeable.'

'Oh.' Uriah frowned slightly, then smiled. 'Have you changed your mind about leaving Jericho with Salmah?'

'What!' Rahab tried to hide her shock. Uriah stopped and took her hand, kissing it gently.

'I was going to ask you to marry me Rahab, until I saw how you looked at Salmah, how you asked for him the moment you awoke.' Uriah let the Priestess's hand go and looked at his feet as an embarrassed boy would.

'Oh Uriah. I have loved you since we were children and if you had asked me a month ago, I would have agreed, but you would not have asked, would you?'

'No.' Uriah moved his feet, but kept his eyes downcast.

'It is amazing how circumstances make us re-evaluate life.' Rahab took Uriah's hand, lent in and kissed him softly on the lips. As she pulled back, she smiled. 'I will marry Salmah and leave with him. He is the leader of his tribe and they will accept my past, even if the Israelites will not. Something you could never do and still reign over Jericho and rule you must.'

'No, I will die and Iki will rule if father does not recover.'

'No, you will live Uriah, you just have to believe.'

'Believe in what?'

'Come with me. I have something you must see.' Rahab clasped the Prince's hand and pulled him down the side alley toward her Inn.

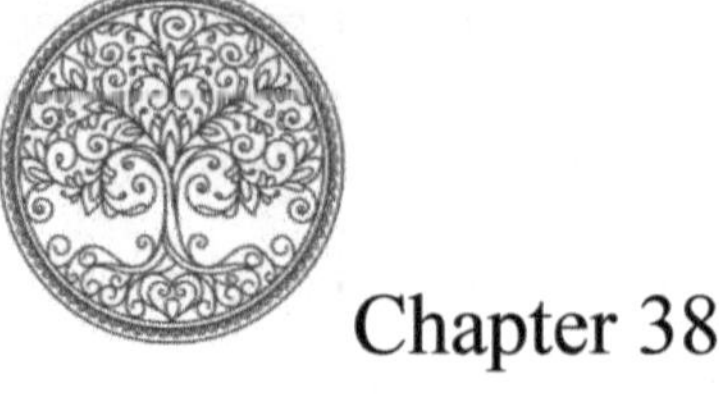

Chapter 38

Danal followed Rahab and Uriah down the cobblestoned alleyway that led to Rahab's Inn. She kept her distance, preferring they did not see her. She had watched the kiss and something inside of her had broken in that moment; the tenderness, the love and care. Rahab had lied to her all this time.

All the talk of taking what she wanted and being in charge. It was all a farce.

The Priestess did not stop at the Inn as Danal expected, instead she carried on past. Danal wanted to confront Rahab, but she could not find the courage. The two had been friends for so long and it puzzled the young woman as to why Rahab would keep her feelings for Uriah hidden. Why not tell everyone how she felt? The deceit was what festered in Danal's heart and try as hard as she did, she could not push the pain down.

They entered the shrine of Asherah and Danal waited outside until she was sure they were far enough in to not see her follow. After a short wait, she slipped past the thick green hedge that marked the entrance and looked for cover. She had not entered the Shrine since Rahab had taken her there so many years before. Nothing had changed, not even the trees had grown bigger. It was as though time stood still in the garden of the Goddess.

Danal began to wonder if Rahab had planned a secret marriage. Why else would she bring Uriah to the Shrine of Asherah? She ducked down behind a large stone statue of the Goddess to wait and watch. Her eyelids felt heavy and a metallic taste began in her throat. A shimmer of light appeared before Rahab as Danal tried to overcome the growing urge to close her eyes and not open them again.

****

'Why have you brought me here Rahab?' Uriah stopped before a wall of carvings. The surface was rough and for a moment he thought it stone until he realised it was made of wood. The images showed the old gods, gathered around a large table overflowing with food in abundance.

'You will see Uriah.'

'You have lost your mind. We have an invasion outside the walls and a traitor about to be arrested and you bring me to your favourite hiding place.'

'The Goddess asked me to bring you.'

'Rahab, you know I am not a believer.'

'You believe the Israelites have a powerful God on their side, but we cannot have the help of a Goddess?'

'No, I believe the Israelites have strong magic working in their favour, how I have no idea'

'So, they survived forty years in the desert, parted the waters of the Jordan, arrived at our walls un-accosted and now make our defences look useless with *magic?* Where do you believe their magic comes from?'

'I have no idea but I would really like to know.' Uriah knew he was in denial over the sights he had seen but since Adon had died, his belief system was more challenged than it had ever been.

'Is there any part of you that can accept they have a God and that my Goddess is real? Look around you and tell me you do not believe.'

Uriah considered Rahab's questions. He could feel the peace the garden offered. All around him the green carpet of grass grew. He wondered over this unique piece of perfection in what was otherwise a dry area, shaded by buildings.

The garden had been at the centre of Jericho for as long as he could remember and his father's father before him. It blossomed all year around and nothing ever withered or died within it. Not that Uriah visited often, but the trees could be seen from the Palace walls. They seemed like patient giants, watching over the city.

'It is not that I do not believe in the old gods Rahab. it is more that we have moved beyond them. We have farming implements, physicians, artists and knowledge. If the gods existed before, then their time is done. We have outgrown them.'

'If what you say is true, then once we grow up and learn what we need to know, we suddenly have no need for our father or mother for we have outgrown them? Is this what you mean?'

'Of course not. We still love them. We still come to their aid when needed. We still care for them in their aging years.'

'Exactly. Just because you have not needed the Goddess does not mean she does not exist. Maybe the Israelites asked their God for help and because they asked he has given them what they desire, our city.'

Uriah was confused. Yes, he had seen the water of the Jordan parted, he had felt the walls begin to crumble, he believed the Israelites would be upon them tomorrow. Why was it so hard for him to believe the Goddess could help his people, if the God of the Israelites was aiding them?

The Prince sank down to his knees as though the weight of the world had descended upon his shoulders. 'How am I to save my people? If what you say is true, all you believe I need to do is call upon the Goddess for help?'

'Exactly so.' Rahab touched Uriah's shoulder as she spoke. 'We are not made to take the burden of our world alone Uriah. Call the Goddess to you.'

'But how?'

'Just as you would call your father for help.'

Chapter 39

Nalia giggled quietly as Iki whispered in her ear. He kissed her neck continuing to watch the tavern for any sign of Nimal. He was trying almost unsuccessfully to stay focussed. Nalia was a terrible distraction. Despite her original offer to provide him with her services for free, he was yet to take advantage of or accept her invitation. There was something magnetic about the woman he had found more exciting than merely getting her into his bed.

'Here he comes.' Iki spoke softly just before kissing Nalia gently on the lips. The young woman kissed his top lip in response sending shivers down his spine. 'Oh, you are in so much trouble when we finish here.'

Nalia's eyes almost sparkled at the idea and Iki forced himself to peek past her thick auburn hair to watch Nimal more closely. Shiba knew Nimal on sight and the moment of truth would come when she served him. Would he recognise her?

****

'What can I get ya mista?' Shiba spoke a more common speech than she generally used. She had removed all the usual eye and lip colour and grubbied her face a little with sweat and soot from the cook fires. She wore a serving apron and plain clothing, nothing like the sheer and exotic clothing Nimal would be acquainted with.

'You can give me a nice sweet ride is what you can do honey.' Nimal pulled Shiba onto his lap and fondled her breasts with his face.

'You gotta buy a drink first mista. No snogging until the bar tab is settled. Them's house rules.' Shiba was starting to get a feel for her character and wondered if she might have missed her vocation. Nimal tossed a coin on the table.

'Then you had best be quick because I have an impressive gift to share with you and it is hot and ready to go.'

Shiba resisted the urge to roll her eyes. If she had a copper for every time she had been told a man's appendage was the best she would ever ride, she would have been retired with servants of her own by now.

Shiba collected up the prefilled mug of ale. The bar keeper nodded as the Priestess prepared herself for the next few minutes of groping.

'Here you go Mista, best brew in the house. Just for you.' Nimal grabbed the ale and took a long swig before Shiba could place it on the table. He seemed to manage to collect the Priestess's arm in the process and swung her around to sit on his lap.

'Have we met before? You look awfully familiar.' Shiba kept her expression calm. Her line of work dictated she develop the best acting skills known to man. There was the *genuine* smile you gave the ugly ones. Of course she could not do her work without the lustful rapture of an orgasm that never existed and there was the look she was using now of *whatever do you mean?*

'Just new here mista so don't think so.'

Nimal seemed to forget his concern as he licked Shiba's neck and began to lift her skirt with his one free hand, the other still firmly holding his ale.

'You betta finish your ale and order another before the boss gets cranky Mista.' Shiba nodded to the mug of ale still in Nimal's hand.

'I can do both.' Nimal smirked and the expression left Shiba a little cold. His hand was working overtime under her skirt but as he took a few more long gulps of his ale it began to have the desired effect.

Shiba pulled Nimal's hand out from under her dress as his face slid by her chest onto the table with a thud. A few patrons looked questioningly at the girl who shrugged, lifted an imaginary mug to her lips and made dizzy crossed eyes.

Iki arrived a few moments later. 'Oh my, Nimal. Looks like you have overdone the ale again. Sorry miss.' Iki nodded to Shiba. 'He just cannot take his ale these days. I think maybe his liver is not the best.' Iki smiled as Nalia joined him in helping lift Nimal from the long wooden bench seat.

'He is really heavy.' Nalia complained quietly. 'How on earth are we going to get him out of here?'

Nimal was less than cooperative and totally unable to move his legs. 'I thought you said the draft would make him drowsy!' Iki frowned. Shiba merely shrugged.

'Rahab organised it, not me.' Shiba whispered. 'Here, let me help ya Mista.' Shiba spoke louder, making a show of assisting the *drunken* Captain from the tavern.

It took a few moments of man handling before Nalia, Iki and Shiba managed to get Nimal into the alley where the Royal guard were waiting.

'Get this ass out of here Commander. I want him chained up in the dungeon. Be quiet about it.' The Prince almost threw the former Captain of the guard at the Commander. 'If he gets a few bruises before I get there, I will not be too worried.' Iki smiled and the Commander nodded his understanding.

'What now?' Nalia watched the guards as they half dragged, half carried Nimal to the Palace dungeon.

'Now, you and I take a walk.'

'Where?'

'So many questions. I believe you will understand when we get there.' Iki grinned mischievously.

Iki took Nalia by the hand and led her across the roadway to the place where they had first met. He guided her past the table where they had waited for Nimal to arrive and then around the bar, collecting a bottle of spirits as they passed then on through the alley and out the back of the building. It did not take long for Nalia to realise where he was taking her.

'You think I owe you a favour good sir?' Nalia curtsied patronisingly.

'Not at all. It is I who owe you a favour my dear and I am very, very good at repaying my debts.'

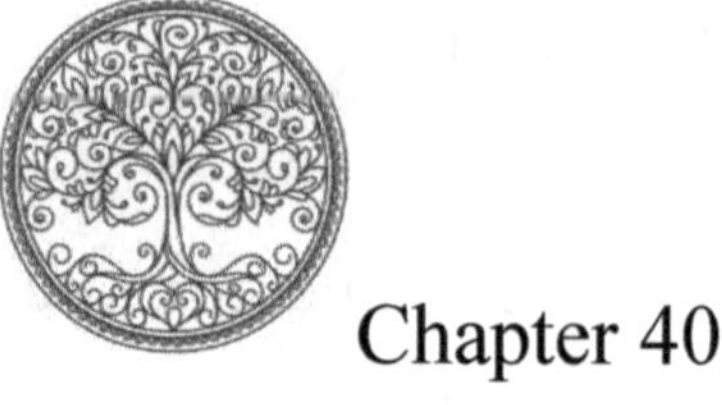

Chapter 40

Asherah watched and waited. She knew Moloch's influence was limited in her Sanctuary and there was no doubt in her mind that her brother had been doing his best to keep the Prince from calling upon her. She had felt Uriah's confusion when the Israelites had crossed the Jordan. She had sensed the surge of curiosity about the divine but he had buried it quickly beneath his frustration and fear.

Uriah was on his knees, Rahab's arm wrapped around his broad shoulders. 'Just ask for Asherah's help.' The Priestess urged.

'I have failed my people Rahab. I am willing to give my life to save theirs.'

'You have no way of knowing if Joshua will accept your offer. Salmah will try Uriah, yet I do not believe peace is what the Israelites seek. Ask the Goddess for guidance if nothing else.'

There was a part of Uriah's soul that longed to beg the Goddess for help, yet there was an inner voice that spoke to him of his failure, of his weakness and frailty. If Rahab was right and Joshua did not accept his sacrifice, then who else was there to save his people?

He had no choice but to have an alternative plan yet all his other avenues were already exhausted. If the older gods existed, then they were playing games with the lives of his people. He was filled with a sense of rage at the thought of such carelessness.

'Rahab I will call upon the Goddess, as you wish, but to answer my questions, not to do my work for me.' Rahab smiled at the Prince. He was always so full of his own importance. Not in a horrible way, but in the way that he thought everything that happened to him was of his own making and under his control. The past week had thrown his world into turmoil.

'Very well. Hold my hand Uriah.' Rahab took the Prince's hand in hers and closed her eyes. She could feel the warmth of his skin and memories flooded her mind. Their first meeting as children, the first time they kissed and then the very first time he took her to his bed.

Uriah had been hers and his role as the Prince and future King of Jericho had taken him from her. She wondered for a moment why she wanted to help save Jericho and then realised she did not. The city was nothing more than walls of rock. She wanted to save the people and most of all, she longed to see Uriah safe.

'What now?' Uriah whispered.

'Now we pray.' Rahab squeezed Uriah's hand reassuringly. 'Asherah I bring you Uriah, son of Hamilkot, Prince of Jericho.'

The darkness of the tree tops opened with overwhelming light as though the sun had suddenly risen in a night sky. The Prince shielded his eyes from the brightness. Beyond the light, he could see waterfalls cascading down invisible mountains into lakes of clear blue water. As the darkness of the shrine withdrew, Uriah felt his body become weightless.

'Say the words Prince.' The voice was almost musical in his mind and Uriah shook his head for clarity. Rahab's hand was still within his but he could not see her. 'Rahab is with you Uriah, but this you must do on your own.'

'I do not understand?' Uriah gasped as he realised he was floating above the waterfalls that sprang from nothingness. 'Where am I?'

'Stop thinking Prince and feel. There are so many parts of life and death that cannot be explained with logic. You saw the River waters cease to flow. You know the power of the Creator.'

'Creator?' Uriah felt like a child lost in a world he had never known.

'The older gods are real Uriah and we serve the Creator, or at least we are called to do so. Not all the older gods serve faithfully. There is so much more I do not have time to show you, but know this, you must live for you serve the Creator's plans.'

'What does He need of me?'

'You need not worry yourself of the how Uriah, or the why. Just follow my directions.'

Uriah pushed the fascination of the Goddess and his surroundings aside. It felt unreal, as though someone was trying to trick him. 'I have offered my life, I gave my word. My death for the lives of my people.'

'Joshua will not accept your offer. Your plan to leave your brother to rule in your place will fail. Your people will be murdered and enslaved.'

'You say the Creator aids the Israelites, yet you serve the Creator and you are helping me. That does not make a lot of sense Goddess.'

Asherah smiled at the Prince but he could not see her face. Only her words filled his mind. 'It is complex Uriah. The Creator aids the Israelites, but he has sent me to ensure your people are safe.'

'It sounds too much like games of earthly politics to be of the gods.'

'We may not be human Uriah, but we all have our own mind. The children of the Creator are powerful, but our Father is more so. Some fear Him, others love Him. I adore Him.' Asherah remained patient. Uriah was an intelligent man and one who used his mind to rule his heart.

'So, what do you want me to do? How will you save my people when the walls fall?'

'You need to trust me Uriah and faith comes before proof. Do you trust me?'

'I am not sure I trust anyone, except possibly Rahab. She believes in you, yet that is not enough for me. I feel like a pawn in a game and it is not a feeling I relish.'

'I understand your confusion, your reservations. Some say our path is laid out before we are even born. Some say the Creator is the only one to know the path, yet it is not the path he knows, it is the destination. How we get there is up to each of us Uriah. We can take the easy way, the hard way or the long way to the destination. I am offering you the easy way; the way that will spare you the pain of losing so much of what you love.'

'If it is alright with you Goddess, I believe I will choose *my* way.'

Chapter 41

Danal awoke feeling heavy. Her mind was foggy with thoughts of betrayal. When she sat up and looked beyond her hiding place, Uriah and Rahab were gone. She was too late. If there had been a marriage ceremony she had missed it, but why had she fallen asleep?

She stumbled as she began to walk from the Shrine. Night had completely enveloped the city and Danal realised that this was the last night before the Israelites claimed they would bring down the walls.

She puzzled over why Rahab and Uriah would choose now to marry. Uriah had offered his life to save his people. If they simply wanted one more night of passion, marriage was unnecessary.

All the years she had waited for Uriah to realise she loved him, to take her as his wife, to be given the chance to rule by his side. She felt humiliated and stupid. She had to find Rahab. The woman had everything she could possibly want, why had she taken Uriah too?

****

Iki watched Nalia as she slept. The sun had set and the barn was now almost dark. It was time to go and the young Prince realised he had no desire to leave Nalia behind. He had no idea what tomorrow would hold. If the Israelites could indeed bring the walls down, if his brother would give his life and he would rule in his place... Now was not the time to overthink the future.

Iki gently touched Nalia's shoulder, nudging her awake. 'We must go now.'

'We, where?'

'Will you marry me this night Nalia?' The barmaid laughed, the sound drifting in the darkness.

'Have you gone mad? You are a Prince; I am barely one class up from a whore. I am fairly sure your brother will have something to say about this.'

'I doubt that. You have met Rahab and my brother has loved her for more years than you could possibly know. Not a day goes by when he does not regret choosing his position over her. This last week has been an eye opener for me Nalia.' Iki stroked her naked arm and lent in to find her lips in the darkness. The smell of her hair, the taste of her flesh and the warmth of her skin were beyond any mere pleasure the young Prince had known, and he had known a lot of pleasure.

'Why me?' Nalia asked huskily between kisses.

'Because you are like no woman I have ever known. You fire my blood, you treat me like I am not a Prince. You see the real me.'

Nalia wrapped her arms around Iki's neck and pulled him close to her. 'I accept your proposal Prince. On one condition.'

'Anything?' Iki breathed.

'If this plan of your brothers goes astray, no heroics. You leave your crown behind and live.'

****

'Uriah, what do you mean? The Goddess has told me, shown me your future. Please listen to her. What did she say?' The Prince turned on Rahab, feeling the fear in her words.

'She told me she was offering me the easy way out of this mess.'

'Then take it. For the sake of all that is holy, please Uriah, take the easy way.'

'You had best make the necessary preparations Priestess. The walls fall tomorrow and your family is spread far and wide around the city. You have the promise of safety. Take it.'

'And why should I accept such a promise when you will not? No Uriah. I will get word to my family, but we have known one another too long for me to leave you to your stupid arrogant ego.'

****

Salmah lay on his bed and waited in his quarters as the last rays of light filtered through his tent walls. Deshaun's pallet remained in their tent and Salmah pondered his loss. *How many more must die Lord before this thirst for power, for property is quenched?*

Salmah felt the weight of his responsibility fall heavily on his shoulders. He was young, very young to be leading a whole tribe of people. He had not even had the chance to speak with his men and this concerned him. Would they kill the innocent children of Jericho or enslave them as Joshua wished? Even if he could speak with them, would he really ask them to betray the will of the anointed leader of the Israelites?

There was a piece of the man that wondered if Rahab had indeed corrupted him. He knew there was likely nothing she asked of him that he would not do, but he also believed she would not ask him to do anything to dishonour his people.

Forty years his people had wandered the desert. For forty years, the Prophet had promised them the land of milk and honey but at no time had the Prophet told them they would take it by force and enslave children. No, it was Joshua who asked this deed of the people and Salmah had to believe his God did not wantonly kill innocents for his own gain.

Salmah swung his legs around and pushed himself to his feet. He walked to the opening of his tent and spoke briefly with the guard who nodded and agreed to his request. He needed to get word to his men if he was going to ensure Joshua did not kill

Uriah and enslave his brother. The old man had forbidden him from leaving but he had said nothing about meeting with his tribal council.

****

'Interesting these humans. I still do not understand why Father wastes so much of his time on them?' Moloch floated beyond the boundary of Asherah's home.

'You are not welcome here Moloch.'

'Oh that I can tell dear sister. The wards you placed are rather electrifying.' The demon smiled in a way that bred distrust. 'It looks like your little plans might be falling apart. That Uriah is a feisty one after all.'

'He has more of his father in him than I first believed but we are not finished here yet Moloch. Father does not want this line to end here today.'

'Maybe he does, maybe he does not, either way it is strange that Father is sending the Israelites in to stamp out those who worship you my dear sister.'

'That is merely what the Israelites believe. What Joshua thinks he knows and what Father wants are two different ideas indeed.' Asherah realised Moloch had baited her into a debate and shook herself free. 'Go away brother. No children will be sacrificed here tomorrow. I will make sure of that.'

'Oh, you will not mind if I hang around on the off chance, will you? Invading soldiers seem to just let their blood lust get away from them you know and I am fairly sure even the Israelites do not know they will be offering up a few morsels to me when the walls fall.'

Asherah ignored her brother but he was right. How could Father allow the invasion to go ahead? She knew all the innocents who died were raised to the heavens but it still did not seem right to take away from them the time they had in the flesh. There were so many wonders to enjoy; this she knew.

Yes, the gods lived forever and the spirits of the dead endured for eternity but the flesh offered joys that could never be understood by the spirit. It took a holistic existence to experience life to the full and taking the lives of children before they grew to adulthood was cruel beyond imagining.

Maybe this experience of life was why the gods envied humanity and often chose to take their form. There was the pleasure of winning a race or the disappointment of losing in games. There was a first crush, first kiss, first time making love, the first child born, the first harvest of the fields, the sweet smell of flowers and the first time to dance to the sound of music.

The spirit could not know these joys as the flesh could and although each soul who departed tomorrow would live for eternity in the Heavens, they may never know these sensations and for that, Asherah was angry with her father.

Asherah had to make sure Uriah lived. Yahweh knew this; he wanted the line to survive so why was he making this so difficult?

Chapter 42

The grey of near dawn covered the Israelite camp as men began to move about in preparation. Salmah had barely slept, his mind racing with thoughts of Rahab and Joshua's betrayal.

A guard still stood outside the tent, ensuring the leader of Judah did not sneak into the city overnight. Joshua was right to expect Salmah to warn Uriah. The man deserved better and Salmah could not help but question Joshua's motives once more.

'It is time Sir.' A young man walked into the tent and it took a moment for Salmah to recognise him.

'Nathan. A beard, it looks good on you cousin.' The young man smiled. 'Are the men ready?'

'They are Salmah. Are you sure this is the right thing to do?'

'No Nathan, I am not sure, but what I do know is that I will not ask my people to follow Joshua any longer. God has granted us our freedom; I cannot believe it was given only to murder and enslave others. God's own laws forbid killing and stealing, yet Joshua demands we do both. It does not seem like an honourable act to me and we will have no part in it.' Nathan nodded his understanding as the sound of trumpets filled the cool morning air.

The guard stood aside as Salmah exited his quarters. 'I think you have better things to do now Isiah.' The guard smiled, bowed his head slightly and left to join the other tribesman lining up behind the Ark of gold.

A wispy white mist began to form around the Israelites and it became difficult to see the walls of the city. Salmah heard more then saw Joshua leave his tent. His voice carried through the thickening fog.

'Today the Lord our God will deliver Jericho into our hands. He will bring down the walls and provide us with prosperous lands filled with people to work the fields and we will rule this nation in his honour. The Canaanites will know the true power of our God and they will tremble. I want every temple and shrine to the pagan gods of the Canaanites destroyed. Follow your kinsmen Israel for today we enter the Promised Land.'

'How long did it take him to rehearse that speech?' Nathan whispered.

'Too long Cousin, too long.'

The Ark began to glow brightly as the sun rose above the walls of the city. The heat slowly burnt off the fog and the eeriness lifted. Salmah looked up to see the walls lined with people. *Oh Lord, please get them down from the walls, please!*

Already men had begun the long walk around the base of the city walls. The trumpets sounded to mark the beginning of the journey, but then Joshua had ordered silence. The men painstakingly took every step carefully in an effort to create a mesmerising march upon the city of Jericho.

Unlike the past six days, on this day the men of Israel would circle the city seven times. Salmah knew it was going to be a long day and he kept an eye out for any opportunity to make his way back to Rahab and warn Uriah of Joshua's plans.

****

'We need to get the people down from the walls Uriah.' Rahab spoke as Iki entered the meeting hall, taking the steps to the lounge area in one leap. Nalia followed a moment later.

'I agree, but how? They are curious beyond belief and even the rumbling of yesterday has not kept them away.'

'They will get down when the cracks appear.' Iki smiled. 'I have Nimal in the dungeon. You said you wanted to question him Rahab.'

'No questions required. I had an idea but your stubborn brother put an end to it.' Rahab scowled at the Prince, who shrugged in answer.

'What do you mean?' Danal entered the meeting hall as Iki spoke.

'They got married. That is what she means.' Iki's eyes opened widely everyone's gaze fell on Danal.

'What are you talking about?' Rahab stood to greet her friend.

'I saw you at the Shrine. What else were you doing there?' Danal had her hands on her hips and was feeling unusually defiant.

'Meeting with the Goddess.' Uriah answered, a slight smile on his face. 'Rahab is marrying Salmah, if he survives the invasion of course.'

'What?' Danal and Iki asked in unison, while Nalia collected a cup of watered wine and sat back to watch the entertainment.

'The Goddess.' Iki almost choked on the fig he had thrown into his mouth moments before.

'Marry the spy.' Danal left her mouth open as though she had seen the dead rising.

Rahab lifted her hand for the conversation to cease. 'We have more important issues than my pending marriage Danal. I have no idea what made you think I was marrying Uriah. You and I need to talk later, but not now.'

'You saw the Goddess?' Iki continued spluttering as he spoke while Nalia passed him her cup smiling.

'I saw the Goddess.' Uriah answered, pouring himself a cup of water.

'That is amazing. What did she want?' Iki was smiling now, his eyes sparkling with excitement. 'Is she as beautiful as the old carvings show? What I would give to meet a Goddess.' Iki flinched as Nalia punched him in the arm.

'She wanted me to leave the city for safety. Something about our line surviving. I told her I had given my word and nothing was changing that.'

'You what?' Iki gaped.

'I know. I told him he was being pig-headed but he would not listen to me.' Rahab tapped her chest as she spoke.

Danal sat down as she swallowed her embarrassment. How could she have just blurted out such a stupid comment in front of everyone, even Iki's concubine? Suddenly, she felt ill.

'The people, off the walls everyone. How are we going to manage it?' Rahab clicked her fingers for everyone's attention.

'We only have the Royal guard left and using force would only cause a riot.' Everyone nodded as Uriah explained.

'We have no use for Nimal now. What about a public trial and possible execution? That will bring everyone off the walls and into the city.' Rahab smiled.

'The Israelites are already circling the city. We do not have much time Rahab.' Uriah rubbed his forehead with the back of his hand.

'Actually, we have all day. I learnt from Salmah a few days ago that the Priests will circle the city seven times on this last day. Apparently, the Israelite God has a fixation with the number seven. We have most of the day to get the people away from the walls and somewhere safe.'

'The Palace will not be safe. It forms part of the wall itself and the training ground and soldier's barracks are too close.' Uriah looked worried.

'What about the garden of Asherah?' Rahab could not explain exactly why she had chosen the garden but now she had said it aloud, it made perfect sense. Uriah would be close to Asherah and if there was any chance to get the man away, she was going to take it, even if she had to knock him unconscious to do it.

'That could work.' Iki looked hopeful. 'There are wide streets leading in. The gardens are huge but will the Goddess be happy if we end up executing Nimal there?

'We will not execute him in the garden itself. We can hold the trial at the market square alongside the gardens. The local merchants will be so busy trying to sell their wares, even more people will be kept from the walls.' Uriah stopped for a moment. 'Many of the people believe Nimal was within his rights to raid the Israelite camp. I am not sure an execution will be the outcome.'

Rahab smiled to herself. Killing simply was not in the man's heart, she knew. 'It is not a matter of if we do or do not execute him Uriah. It is the thought of it that will bring the people flocking and that will keep them safe, for now.'

'And if Joshua accepts my offer, they will all remain safe.' Uriah seemed content with his decision.

Chapter 43

The plan had seemed simple enough. In the confusion, Salmah's men would cover his escape but as the arrow narrowly missed his leg, he could not help but wonder if a more complex plan may have been a better option.

He scrambled over the edge of the window and thanked God that Rahab had left the rope out. He fell on the floor with a loud thud that was shortly followed by Musaf appearing in the wash room doorway along with some faces Salmah had never seen.

The cook walked over and helped the spy to his feet, gently touching the bruise on the young man's face and frowning his concern. 'You took your time. What happened to you?'

'This,' Salmah pointed to his wounds, 'Uriah, well a few guards in truth, but it is all sorted now.'

'Ah, fighting over Rahab.' The cook nodded knowingly.

'No, just fighting.' Musaf laughed and slapped Salmah on the back.

'The family are all here as Rahab requested.' Salmah looked around realising who the new faces must belong to.

'Where is Rahab? What do you mean she requested?'

'She sent word that you might return, that her family should gather. Shiba spent most of the night collecting everyone up.'

'So, if Rahab is not here, where is she?'

'With Uriah at the Palace.' Salmah moved past the cook, out into the main dining area and jostled his way through the throng of activity before him. He had no time to introduce himself, he had to find Rahab before the walls fell.

'That damned woman.' Salmah spoke aloud. All she had to do was join her family in the safety of her home and she would live but no, she was off trying to save Uriah.

As he moved out into the street he saw people climbing down from the walls, all making their way to the centre of the city. He knew he could not ask anyone what was going on, his accent was too strong and he did not want to be detained by anyone. He needed to find Rahab.

Instead he listened carefully to the chatter. There was talk of a trial or execution, of retribution for the Prince's death. A large gathering was at the garden and marketplace. It did not take him long to realise that Uriah would be at the gathering and where ever Uriah was, Rahab would not be far away.

The crush of people was almost suffocating. He felt like a herded animal as the people all milled around trying to find a good place to see the trial. Children climbed onto their father's shoulders, people stood on tables and others climbed walls and sat on stall awnings for a better view.

Uriah and Iki led out the prisoner as all the people jeered and laughed. 'This man, Nimal, former Captain of the city guard is accused of leading an unsanctioned revolt into the Israelite encampment.' A cheer rose as Uriah hushed the crowd with his hand. 'No friends. We were on the verge of peace and this man led Prince Adon into a trap. The Prince is dead because this man over-stepped his rightful place as a city guard. He led his men into peril and they all died, except him.'

A hush fell upon the crowd as they absorbed the information. Uriah was a great speaker, no wonder he chose politics over fighting Salmah smiled to himself.

He had to get to Rahab, to tell her that when the walls fell, they would all die if they did not prepare to fight. He could not think of any other answer. The people were now down from the walls, they would not die in the crush of stone and rubble but when the men of Israel breeched the walls, they had orders to kill, not negotiate peace with Uriah.

Salmah skirted around the outside of the crowd. The hedge of the garden of Asherah ran down the right side of the market square and no one stood within the garden itself. He did not feel comfortable entering the shrine without Rahab, but it was the only way to get to her without climbing over every man, women and child of Jericho.

Salmah pushed his way to the edge of the garden and tried to find an opening in the hedge. The wall of trees was almost solid and it took some time to realise that going under was the only option.

He dropped to his belly pulling himself under the dense shrubbery. Slowly he shimmied along the ground until he entered the garden. A sense of calm touched him then and as he stood he was greeted by a woman with golden hair and crystal green eyes.

'Salmah. It is good to meet face to face at last.'

'Who are you?' Salmah took a step back, trying to decide if the woman posed a threat or not.

'I mean you no harm. You and I will get to know each other more in time, but for now, you have work to do.' The woman smiled with genuine care and Salmah relaxed.

'I am sorry, but I need to speak with someone.'

'I know. You must bring the people to me Salmah. I have opened my sanctuary and found a place for everyone.'

'I am sorry, I think you have me mixed up with someone else.' Salmah tried to be polite, but the woman was rambling like a simpleton.

'I am Asherah. You and I know Joshua will not let anyone live. Bring them all to me Salmah and they will live. The people of Canaanite deserve life as do the Israelites.'

'How? How could you know what Joshua is planning? How can you save thousands of people?'

'You have faith Salmah. I have heard your prayers, so has Father. Have faith now. Convince Rahab and Uriah to bring the people to me, all of them.'

Salmah backed away from the Goddess. His mind was racing as the blonde woman shimmered and disappeared. How could the Goddess know the God of his people? How could they be helping one another when the history of his people showed that God punished those who worshipped other gods?

It made no sense; it had to be a trick, but now was not the time to dwell on such matters. Asherah was offering safety and accepting it was a risk he had to take. Salmah took a deep breath and turned to find a way out, a way to Rahab.

There was only one entrance into the garden and it was blocked with a milling crowd. Salmah listened for Uriah's voice and followed the sound to the far corner of the hedge of trees.

He was close, but not close enough. He had no choice but to crawl under the garden hedge once more. He found himself in an alleyway behind a row of market stalls. All eyes were on the trial, so Salmah made his way toward the Royal family. The guards were tightly packed around the Prince, shields linked and soldiers facing outwards. Salmah scanned the men.

His eyes finally fell upon the Commander of the Royal guard. He did not know his name but if anyone was going to let him get word to Rahab, it would be the Commander.

Salmah pushed his way carefully through the people. Emotions were running high as some questioned the trial of the city's Captain. He was known to many and although he might not have instilled love in all hearts, he likely had a network of associates who would not want to see him executed.

Uriah continued to state his case, explaining to the people how strange it was that Nimal had been the sole survivor, how Adon was a fighting man and that Nimal should have known better than to lure him into combat.

Salmah wondered over the trial. He knew he was responsible for Adon's death, no one else. Why was Uriah putting the Captain on trial? Almost everyone in the city was trying to get a glimpse of the proceedings.

Salmah reached the Commander who did not recognise him at first. 'I need to talk with Rahab. The Israelites are coming.'

'We know they are coming. You helped them, remember.' The Commander remained calm, eyes forward and at full attention.

Salmah knew any talk of the Goddess would be futile and the Commander did not seem to take the threat of his people seriously. 'You know I killed

Adon, not Nimal. Do you really want to see him executed?'

The Commander looked to Nimal standing beaten and bloodied on a raised platform for all to see. 'I never did like the man.'

'Please, just ask Rahab to come to speak with me. It is important. You must have heard Uriah has offered his life for the people.' The Commander stopped gazing straight ahead and looked down at Salmah. He stood at least a head taller as nearly all the Royal Guard did. It was as though they were carefully chosen for their extraordinary height.

'Rahab, and only Rahab.' The Commander indicated for the man either side of him to close the gap he vacated.

Salmah could see nothing while he waited but he heard the rumbling before he felt the ground move. He was running out of time. Rahab appeared inside the perimeter of Royal Guards and when she recognised him, forced her way past the guards through to him. 'We do not have long. I need to speak with Uriah.' Rahab frowned but did not argue.

The Commander had returned to take his place in the protective line surrounding the proceedings. Rahab turned back to the barricade and the Commander. 'Let me through to Uriah's Commander.' The man stepped aside to allow the Priestess access, Salmah followed closely. Turning to Salmah so he could hear her over the crowd Rahab spoke. 'What is it Salmah?'

Salmah lent forward closing the gap between them. 'Long story, but Joshua plans to kill Uriah and enslave or kill everyone else. You must warn him. Believe it or not, the Goddess tells me she can save everyone.' Rahab stopped moving forward and Salmah nearly bumped into her.

'The Goddess?'

'Yes, Uriah first.' Salmah pointed ahead to the Prince. 'Then I will explain.'

Rahab reached the platform and signalled for Iki to come over. Uriah continued to outline Nimal's offences, but he caught sight of his brother moving toward Rahab and raised a questioning eyebrow.

'Salmah needs to speak with Uriah. Can you take over this charade?' Iki smiled at Rahab's reference to their theatrics and turned to approach his brother.

'I have an idea.' He whispered in Uriah's ear. 'Rahab needs to speak with you. Trust me, I think I can turn the tide on this trial.' Another rumble rippled through the city and the people looked around nervously as Uriah left the podium and Iki took over proceedings.

'We have the people away from the walls, now we need to keep them from running when the walls come down.' Uriah looked pleased as he spoke with Salmah.

'No Uriah. Joshua has no intention of letting the people live. Those he does not kill, he will enslave.

 Chapter 44

Nathan knew it was nearly time. He hoped Salmah knew what he was doing. The Ark reached the end of its final journey around the city walls and was met with the tail end of soldiers.

Nathan waited, knowing what was to come next. He watched Joshua raise his arm and the trumpets began to sound, followed by the roar of thousands of Israelites. The earth shook with the wave of power that was released and large sections of the city walls began to fall.

Boulders thudded down all around the men of Judah, narrowly missing many. Nathan called for his men to pull back from the walls. The height was immeasurable and the long distance meant pieces of stone landed heavily and rolled long distances before coming to rest. He had no intention of losing anyone to a falling rock. Salmah had been very clear about what they were to do and he had no plans to let his cousin down.

They had talked at length about Salmah's decision to return to the city and although Nathan was not entirely sure why, he had to admire his cousin's conviction.

Joshua had called the Ark back to safety, away from the city accompanied by the Priests, while the men drew their weapons expectantly.

Clouds of dust wafted high into the air, creating a choking haze that obscured the view of the city walls. For a moment, it seemed like the sun was setting as shadows of men danced back and forth and the crash of falling debris continued, increasing in intensity.

The rain of stone persisted as the pile of rubble grew before the men of Israel. Nathan's ears were ringing by the time the haze of dust began to settle and the rumbling sounds subsided.

The soldiers began the climb through and over what was once a barrier to their conquest. Large numbers of casualties had been expected but as

Nathan moved forward he noticed almost no one had fallen with the walls.

Nathan knew exactly where he needed to be. The only place left standing appeared like a tower in the middle of the broken and battered landscape. It would take some time to reach the Inn, but at least Joshua had kept his word. The house of Rahab was left untouched by the carnage. Now it was Nathan's responsibility to ensure no one within was harmed. He had promised Salmah and he intended to keep that promise.

****

Danal did not understand why, but Uriah had sent word for her to take Hamilkot to the Sanctuary of the Goddess. Danal had no way of asking any questions. The message was delivered by two soldiers who advised they would carry the King's stretcher and asked her to bring a physician, anyone but Malic.

The soldiers were running now as rubble exploded from the walls of the Palace. The dark green heavy curtains that hung from the windows along the corridor ripped and shredded as stone and wooden beams fell. The beautiful stone carvings that lined the hallways had cracks appearing and Danal felt her palms go clammy with fear.

It was true, the walls were coming down, but how? The city of Jericho had stood for so many generations and each of those years had been ruled by Hamilkot's ancestors. Now the city was being invaded by foreigners who had the power of the gods on their side.

Danal was not sure if she should cry or scream in rage. Both emotions were running through her mind as the physician fell in front her, tripping her to the ground.

The soldiers waited for no one. Their orders were to bring the King to safety. Danal felt dizzy and disorientated. She rolled onto all fours, crawling toward the physician to help him to his feet. As Danal rolled the man over, she gasped. A sliver of wood had pierced his eye. His other eye lay open looking at the falling ceiling absently.

Danal shook her head, pushing the fear away and forcing the dizziness to leave her. Her body felt stiff and the grazes on her hands were bleeding. The halls were filling with dust and debris and the young noble woman could not see which way the soldiers had gone.

Out of the haze, Danal felt someone grasp her arm. Her heart leapt as she struggled to free herself. *The Israelites could not be here already. The walls still stood.* 'Danal, it is me, Nalia. Iki sent me back with the soldiers to get you. Take my hand.'

Relief flooded her mind. 'What is going on?'

'No time to explain now. The Palace is falling apart. Follow me.' Nalia dragged Danal through the twisting and turning corridors. The dizziness had returned and Danal had no idea where she was. She had lived in and around this Palace nearly all her life and for the first time ever, she felt entirely lost.

'How are you able to find your way?' Danal choked on the dusty air.

'So many questions. No time, we need to run!' Nalia picked up the pace as rubble fell from every wall. The rugs, paintings and mosaic tiles were flying in all directions and the women ducked down as they navigated the darkening hallways.

The sight of open air greeted them both as they sucked in desperate breaths. Danal turned around to see the entrance collapse behind them, a plume of dust exploded from the opening, knocking both women to the ground.

A large crack appeared in the yard, running toward the women at speed. 'Danal, get out the way!' Nalia jumped to her feet and pushed Danal away from the chasm that opened through the Palace steps and out into the parade ground beyond.

'We have to get out of here, now!' Nalia dragged Danal to her feet once more and headed for the street leading to the garden of the Goddess. 'Keep up Danal. There is very little time left.' Nalia was light and agile and fitter than Danal and began to draw away from her rapidly.

Danal was confused but she pushed her anxiety aside as fear grew. Nalia had already disappeared around the corner of a low building into the cobblestone street that led to the market square.

'Get the people into the garden.' Uriah pointed to the hedge past the market stalls as the ground shook more fiercely. The Commander of the Royal guard responded without question.

'No Uriah. You need to get to the Sanctuary of the Goddess first.' Rahab looked concerned, but the Prince ignored her protest.

'Salmah, take Rahab to the Inn, she will be safe there.'

'I am not sure anyone *takes* Rahab anywhere. You of all people should know that.' Salmah looked worried, but both men knew the Priestess was not one to be argued with.

'Where is father?' Uriah called to Iki.

Iki was just about to search for the guards when they appeared, running through the streets. Hamilkot bounced about on the stretcher, blissfully unaware of the commotion. As the guards drew up in front of the Prince everyone could see the dust and debris covering them from head to toe.

'The Palace has fallen Sir.' Uriah acknowledged the guard with a sombre nod.

'Take the King to the garden of the Goddess.' The Prince looked around as the men began to move. 'Where is Danal?'

The guards stopped and looked behind them as though the thought had not occurred to them. 'Not sure Sir. She was there when we were running but to be honest, your orders were clear. Bring the King to the garden no matter what Sir.'

They were right of course, but Danal! 'Carry on.' Uriah looked to Iki.

'On my way brother.' He knew Nalia had returned to help Danal and the feeling in his stomach was something he had never experienced before. The thought of anything happening to Nalia was impossible to consider. The young Prince pushed on ignoring his fears as he retraced the guards' likely route to the Palace.

Chapter 45

'What do you mean the walls were empty!'
Joshua listened to the report from the young man of
the Levite tribe.

'Just that, there was no one on them.'

'Have you taken the King and Princes hostage
yet?'

'No Sir, the Palace has fallen and no one can
get inside but they would have fled to safety. We have
not found them yet.'

Joshua attempted to hide his surprise but the
agitation was showing. Where were they? The Lord
had promised to offer Jericho into his hands, into the
hands of the people of Israel. The Canaanites had to
pay for their past. Surely it was as God had intended.

'Find them, quickly.' Joshua barked at the boy
who leapt to carry out his orders.

The old man wanted to enter the city more than
anything at that moment, but the rubble was too high

for a man of his age and the gates were not yet passable. It would take hundreds of men hours to clear the way for the Priests along with the women and children to enter Jericho.

For now, all he had to go on were the reports coming from the leaders of the twelve tribes and he knew he was not being told everything.

He often wondered why God had named the twelve tribes of Israel. Why not simply create one nation under one ruler? With twelve leaders, it was almost impossible to get anything done satisfactorily.

Walls continued to collapse as men risked their lives to climb into the city as quickly as possible. The spoils would be great from a city as prosperous as Jericho, but they had no idea that all the wealth found within was to be taken by the Priests to establish the religious order that would be the foundation of the Israelite nation.

No, men would be given land and food and slaves to toil for them. A small amount of coin would be given to all who chose to settle in the area, but the remainder of the men would be enlisted to conquer the surrounding lands. For that they would earn a wage and the wealth of Jericho would fund the invasion of the entire Canaanite nation.

****

Asherah focused her energy. The gateway would pass through her sanctuary and on into the lands far to the north of Jericho. The new nation would be founded in a vast area of rugged country that lay nestled between the Great Sea all the way to the Euxine Sea.

'You are interfering sister.'

'Not now Moloch.' Asherah tried to ignore her brother, breathing deeply she felt her fingers tingle with the power of creation.

'You believe you know what Father wants.'

'No, I believe Father loves all of humanity and any life lost is painful for Him.'

'Then why did he bring down the walls of Jericho?'

'To prove a point, who knows Moloch. That is not my problem right now. Go away!' The Goddess struggled to compose herself. Moloch had entered her sanctuary only because her energy was focussed elsewhere.

To banish him, she had to divert her power back to the shield she usually placed around her home to protect it from being seen by the inhabitants of Jericho and to keep unwanted visitors out, yet to do so would lower the energy she could direct towards the rift she now created.

'Very well sister. It is you who must explain yourself to Father when all this is over, not me.' Moloch shrugged and disappeared from the Oasis above the garden of the Goddess.

Asherah let out an audible sigh and returned to her work. The people below could not see the face of the Goddess, but they could now see the cascading waterfalls, the glistening sky and the brilliant light that filtered down to the earth below. There was no need hiding her divinity this day for all who passed into safety would know they had been blessed.

The Goddess looked for Uriah but he had not yet come. Instead, his father Hamilkot lay unconscious on a stretcher. Asherah was tempted to awake him and reveal herself for Hamilkot was a man of humanity worth spending time with, but now was not that time.

Asherah relaxed her mind to allow her power to grow, but her thoughts were wandering. She forced the doubts raised by Moloch aside for they were a debate for another day.

For now, she could be sure that at least Hamilkot would be safe but it was his son who must come through the gateway for it is he who would continue the line that was to aid the future of humanity, a future where peace may truly reign forever on the earth and in Heaven as the Father had intended.

Asherah considered calling upon her brothers and sister but not all would agree and there was no time. All she could do was keep the gateway open for as long as possible and hope that all who needed to pass would find their way.

The Goddess reached out with her spirit to the north. There was a place there she knew and the feeling of the earth called to her. Particles of what seemed like nothingness sparkled in the air as the fabric of space moved at her command.

For the people who watched on from below, the light that sprang from Asherah's fingertips looked like streaks of lightning across the sky. The absence of thunder did not escape them and many watched on nervously.

The walls beyond had fallen and soldiers were pouring in from everywhere. Asherah knew time was running out and her mind raced as the gateway finally opened. A surge of air blew through the gardens like a sandstorm and the people screamed and panic ensued, until a voice came from behind them, it was Uriah.

'Do not be afraid. We have seen the power of the God of Israel, let us now embrace the power of our Goddess. She has promised us safety. Go forward. Leave the fallen walls of Jericho behind.'

The people needed no further encouragement as the sound of swords clashing from beyond the garden rang out.

Chapter 46

Iki drew his sword as the sound of fighting reached him. He could only hope he was headed in the right direction to find his wife. The couple had married after they left the barn the night before and he had not even had the chance to share his good news with Uriah.

The Prince heard a scream, followed by a curse and the noise led him down a laneway that went to the marshalling area near the Palace. Nalia was keeping two soldiers at bay with a long training staff and Danal had a bag full of sling stones and she was throwing them randomly at the men.

Iki drew his sword and ran full speed, 'Step aside Nalia.'

'I have the right, you take the left.' His wife responded defiantly keeping the one man occupied while Iki despatched the first, then the second.

'Quickly, Danal you go first.' Iki helped his friend to her feet.

'Give me that sword; you are going to have to carry her.' Iki nodded handing his sword to his wife before hoisting Danal over his shoulder without reservation. He took off at a run, Nalia following closely behind with staff and sword in hand.

They returned to Uriah with soldiers right behind them. The Royal guard opened their makeshift fortress, allowing the Prince to enter before closing behind him with a precision only practice could afford. 'You need to go brother.' He called out. 'Take father with you and go now, before it is too late.'

'I will not leave you brother.' The Prince moved forward to help Danal down. He looked at her questioningly and she smiled through her dizziness. Satisfied she was alright, he returned his gaze to Iki. 'I am staying right here until every man, woman and child is through that gateway.' He drew his sword and pushed his way back into the market place.

Salmah joined the Prince, his spear at the ready. Rahab collect up a wooden club from a market stall.

Iki retrieved his sword from Nalia who kissed him on the cheek. 'I will look after Danal.'

'You already have lovely lady. Thank you.'

They did not engage the soldiers of Israel, for the Royal guard still maintained a perimeter around the garden entrance. A side alley was overflowing with people who pushed and shoved their way forward, trying desperately to reach what they could not see but instinctively knew represented safety.

An Israeli soldier pushed through the barrier and lunged his spear toward Uriah. Salmah block the blow and landed a heavy punch to the man's head. He slumped heavily to the ground. The young leader of Judah prayed he would not need to take the life a kinsman this day, but the evacuation was moving so slowly.

He looked over his shoulder at the crowds of people who still waited to pass through the gateway. He shook his head at the thought of moving from one place to another, thousands of parasa away within the blink of an eye. When the Goddess had explained it to him, he could hardly believe it but now people slowly filtered into the garden and they were not returning.

'Iki, take Danal and Nalia through.' Uriah pointed toward the line of people that remained.

'I am not leaving you Uriah. I have been through enough this day without losing you all over again.' Danal was close to tears but pushed on. 'I have no idea if you still love Rahab,' Danal looked at the Priestess who nodded her encouragement, 'but I do not care. When this is all over, and it will be over, you are going to marry me. Me! You understand? I almost died trying to get back here after bringing your father to you, I have watched jealously for years wondering when you might finally….' Danal's words were cut off as Uriah's lips closed over hers.

The moment lasted only a heartbeat. 'You are right. I have been foolish.'

'You have? Yes, you have.' Danal regained her composure. Uriah lent in to wipe away a tear that had run down her face during her frustrated tirade. Danal wrapped her arms around the Prince's neck and kissed him passionately. Uriah held his sword arm stiffly for a moment before dropping his sword to the ground and taking Danal in his arms.

'Finally.' Rahab hugged her two most favourite people in the world.

'I hate to interrupt but I am not going anywhere either.' Nalia broke the mood. 'But can someone give me a weapon because the guards seem a little pressed now and we look like we are running out of time.'

Uriah bent down to collect his weapon as two soldiers broke through the shield wall. The small group was pressed backwards against the hedge to the Goddess's garden.

'We could use one of those miracles from the Goddess about now you know.' Iki smiled as he broke his attacker's spear and lunged his sword into the man's exposed belly.

'I think She is otherwise occupied brother. This one is on us.'

'Well that is damned inconvenient.'

A loud commotion began from the far side of the market square. There was no way for the small band of defenders to know what was happening.

Before them a wall of Royal guards were surrounded by hundreds of invaders.

They could hear the clash of weapons and their attackers looked confused. 'Are we expecting reinforcements?' Iki asked his brother as one more invader pushed past the Royal guard.

'None that I am aware of, but let us not refuse their courtesy.'

Salmah caught sight of Nathan for only a moment and he realised who had come to their aid. 'Maybe it is my God you need to thank for this miracle my friends.' Iki and Uriah frowned in confusion. 'Men of Gad and Rueben. The walls have fallen, your role in this is done. The men of Judah fight with me on this. No more killing this day in the Lord's name.'

The clash of swords continued until a large bearded man who was faced off against the Commander of the Royal guard called out in reply. 'We will pull back if your men lower their weapons.'

The clash of weapons slowed but continued. 'If our guards drop their weapons, they will die then we will die shortly afterwards.' Iki whispered to Uriah.

'No, the men who face us never wanted to join this fight. Trust me on this. Joshua forced them to join. They gave their word that they would help but only until the walls of Jericho fell.' Salmah tried to explain. 'Please, my men are dying out there too.'

Uriah bit his lip as he considered his options. They were few and far between. Less than half his people had cleared the garden wall and he had no doubt the Goddess was doing all she could.

They were going to die soon anyway, so he really had nothing left to lose. 'Every man here, on either side, take a step to your rear. Open the space between my guards and your invaders and we agree.'

'You heard the man. Men of Gad, men of Reuben retreat one step now.' Silence filled the streets almost instantly and men looked from one another, shrugging as though a game of sport had ended.

'Lower your weapons Commander.' Uriah ordered, nodding as the Commander looked to him to be sure it was not a trick.

'You heard the Prince men. Lower your weapons.' The guard moved in unison, years of drills and combat evident in every move they made. Their swords were sheathed in one smooth rasp, followed by the sound of one stride backwards.

Salmah pushed past the guards to reach the bearded leader of Gad. He was a big man, with menacing eyes but Salmah had known him all his life. 'Joshua will not be happy my friend but you honoured his orders.'

'We certainly did Salmah. I will take my men home, to our families and the land we were promised beyond the Jordan. A land taken by force is cursed in my mind in any case.'

'You may be right in that Lavon. Judah will be taking our allocation of land and parting ways with Joshua.'

'A wise move on your part boy. I think he lost his mind in the desert, but those walls coming down like that, got to admit that was one amazing sight to behold.'

'It was a show of power, of that you can be sure, but inside those walls of shrubbery right there,' Salmah pointed beyond the garden of the Goddess, 'the people of Jericho are passing across the land, a hundred-day march away to safety all in a heartbeat. I cannot wait to tell Joshua all about it.'

'You might be waiting a while. We have nearly every Levite trying to clear away the rubble from the city gates to let the old bastard in. It will be nightfall before he graces the city proper.'

'Thank you Lavon. That is good news. Do you think the other tribes will be an issue?'

'Not at all. Leave your men and mine to encircle this area until the people are safe. If anyone tries to enter, we will tell them the people are already gone and our tribes are collecting up the wealth.'

Uriah overhead the exchange and moved forward. 'Thank you for allowing my people life.'

'We are all people seeking to provide for our families the best that we can Prince. Death does not provide more food for my children or stronger livestock for breeding. Your city wealth on the other hand, that will come in handy.' Lavon smiled, slapped Salmah on the back and turned to leave. 'With me men of Gad.'

Chapter 47

The last of the people had entered the gateway.

'It is time to go Uriah. The Goddess is tiring, I can feel her pain.'

'I am going to miss you Rahab. I am sorry it took me so long to believe in Asherah, so long to do so many things.'

'You have Danal and Iki and it looks like Iki has Nalia. You are destined for greatness or so Asherah tells me.'

'Be happy Priestess. You deserve it.' Uriah hugged Rahab and kissed her passionately one last time. Danal and Salmah waited a few steps away, allowing them their privacy.

'I am happy Uriah.' Rahab held the Prince at arm's length a moment longer, before turning to hug Danal.

'Thank you Rahab, you opened my eyes to an inner strength I did not know I had.'

'It is often difficult times that bring out the depths of our power Danal. Look after him, he still means a lot to me. I know you understand.'

'I do Rahab, I do. There are some things that cannot be explained and the bond you have shared all these years is one such mystery.'

'He loves you, you do know that?' Rahab reassured her friend.

'Yes, I believe that he does.'

Salmah waited for Rahab to hug Iki and Nalia. The past few days had been overwhelming and he longed to hold her in his arms, to feel her wrapped around his body but there was more that needed to be done before he could focus on Rahab.

Rahab held out her hand to him as her friends turned around for one final wave. The shimmering pond of what appeared to be water absorbed them. It hovered in the air for a few moments before blinking out of existence. Salmah wrapped his arm around the woman who would be his wife and held her as the tears fell.

There was nothing he could say to take away the pain she was feeling in that moment, but he prayed she would find happiness with him and his people now.

'What in God's name is going on Salmah? Where is the Prince, where are all the people of Jericho?' Joshua walked into the garden and stopped when he saw the Priestess in Salmah's embrace. 'Your men said you were busy and tried to bar my entry, but this is not the time or the place to be whoring Salmah.'

Salmah put his finger on Rahab's lips for he knew Joshua's words had ignited her spark. He smiled at her and whispered in her ear. She relaxed and moved away to collect up some precious artefacts from the Shrine of Asherah.

'I will let your disrespect of my fiancé slide old man but it will be the last time, you understand?'

'You should be careful Salmah. It is I who lead the Israelites, not you boy.' Joshua straightened himself up and puffed out his chest as though he could hide his years with such a stance. 'You are yet to explain where the Royal family is being held. All I could find in the city are those in the Inn of your…*fiancé* and one prisoner outside who keeps rambling on about being left behind.'

'Yes, that is the traitor who invaded our camp. He is the reason that Prince Adon died, so you can imagine that the Royal family was a little upset with him.'

'Where are the Princes? I have tribes of men who need something to take their mind off the fact they cannot keep the wealth of Jericho.'

'What do you mean they cannot keep the wealth? You promised them a land of milk and honey and the bounty of a fallen city.' Salmah was not surprised but he was annoyed.

'God promised them prosperity. He promised Israel would rule over the Canaanite lands. I did not promise them the spoils of the invasion, those go to God and God alone. Now answer my question, where are the King and his sons.'

They are gone Joshua, along with all the people who survived the collapse of the walls.' Salmah smiled as he spoke and the look unnerved Joshua.

'That is impossible. We have thousands of soldiers surrounding the city, inside and out. There is no escape.'

'It seems that our God was with us in bringing down the walls of Jericho but in killing and enslaving innocent people, well it appears you may have misinterpreted His prophecy.' Salmah was enjoying this moment, savouring it, ensuring it lasted for as long as possible.

Rahab had removed a layer of her clothing and wrapped some ornately carved pieces from the Shrine. She wished she could take the carved and painted walls, but knew that she could not.

The Goddess would see them reproduced when the time came but for now, she was likely creating a new Sanctuary wherever she had taken Uriah and the people of Jericho for after today's display, they were going to worship her forever.

The Priestess had carefully stayed away allowing Salmah the pleasure of revealing the events to Joshua, but now she could not help but come close enough to overhear.

'What are you talking about Salmah, there must be tunnels below the city, some escape the people had prepared so they could hide and confuse us. I will send men to find them.'

'You will be wasting your time Joshua. I saw the people leave myself.'

'And you did not stop them?'

'Why would I? You have your city; your example of God's power is done. The people of Jericho are free and we have the land promised to us by God. The prophecy is fulfilled and humanity lives on. You know God created all of us, every man, woman and child. The Canaanites were our ancestors, you said so yourself. I am guessing if God created them, he does not really want to see them destroyed.'

'What have you done Salmah? You have ruined God's plans and he will make an example out of you.'

Joshua was growing pale as the vein in his neck pulsed erratically.

'No, you are wrong Joshua. It is God who led the people from here. He sent the Goddess to save them all. It was amazing to see, just as magnificent as the walls falling with a mere trumpet blast, the Goddess opened a gateway that led the people of Jericho to fulfil another prophecy, one he did not see the need to share with you.'

'Take your people and your pagan whore and leave Salmah, you are banished from Israel.' Joshua pointed angrily at the exit to the Shrine of Asherah. When Salmah did not move, he pointed again.

'I will collect our lands first Joshua. As we agreed, I accept the lands south of Jericho and west of the river Jordan. You can carry on wherever you like from here but the tribe of Judah will stay. You see God has revealed a prophecy to me old man and it is one that will shake the foundations of Israel.

# Epilogue

Uriah closed his eyes and Danal held his hand. 'Stay with me my husband. Please do not leave.'

'The Goddess will watch over you and the children Danal. Listen for her voice for she has guided me well.'

'No, it cannot be your time. Not now, not ever. Iki, do something.' Danal could not bear to lose Uriah. Yes, they had enjoyed many years together since they had crossed the gateway, but he was so fit and still young. There was so much good left for him to do.

'I wish I could Danal. The blade must have been poisoned. There is nothing the physicians can do.' Iki had removed the strange looking weapon when he had found it buried in his brother's chest. It was silver but at times flickered in a way that made it almost disappear. A light seemed to shine from inside the hilt but the closer he studied the weapon, the more elusive it became.

As he had touched the spiral hilt, images had flashed before his eyes. He quickly covered the weapon in thick leather and wrapped it up tightly, tying the skin in place with a cord. He could not explain exactly why, but he felt it was dangerous, not only for its sharp blade but there was something else about it he could not explain.

****

Asherah watched on helplessly. Healing was forbidden for all but the Creator himself. Her tears rained down on the city of Hattusa and the people wondered over such an unseasonal downpour.

'I cannot believe you did this Moloch. You are never supposed to meddle with time. Why?'

'There is no rule that says I cannot. You moved these people here across an entire continent. Why can I not move an object through time, just once in a while?'

'Because it was not Uriah's time.'

'It is nothing, his children are alive, all are born to fulfil your silly prophecy. I have not interrupted Father's plans, if they are indeed His plans. What are you so upset about?'

'I am upset because your meddling could alter everything. Look around you, Danal is distraught, Iki has touched the dagger and Uriah's sons will grow up without the love and attention they deserve.'

'There are more surprises up my sleeve you know.' Moloch smirked as he lifted his imaginary sleeve on his dark, almost blood red skin. This red monster was his favourite form and Asherah loathed it.

'Go away. Why Father does not strike you down is beyond me. Your blood lust is insatiable and your moral code is non-existent.'

'That my dear sister is a matter of opinion. I play my part in the plan, just as you do. You may not understand me, but balance is precarious. You think good is always right, but sometimes, in order to do what is right, you must be bad.'

Dedication

When I started writing I was inspired to write, but still finding my own personal style. I believe *The Jericho Prophecy* has seen the best of my work so far. I owe that success to my beta team; my husband George and friend Rachel along with all the awesome emails, reviews and support from readers so far. I'm looking forward to many more books in this new series; each a stand-alone but with the same underlying tone.

What Next!

Deliah and the Dark God, is book 2 in *The Eternal Realm* Series, so why not jump right in and find out how Asherah protects the prophecy from Moloch's meddling.

If you would like to stay up to date with all my latest releases, then joining my mailing list is a great place to start.

Start your journey today with book 1 – *Destiny of Kings* free. Just join my mailing list at www.atime2write.com.au and I will send you a free e-book version.

To find out more about my current work, you can follow me on Facebook or find me on my website www.atime2write.com.au

Thanks again for reading.

Reviews!

Please share your thoughts about *The Jericho Prophecy* by leaving a review with your e-book or paperback seller. It's always great motivation to keep my focus on writing more books when I hear what readers have to say.